HE'S Facing
SEX
Evolution

HE'S Facing
SEX
Evolution

CHUCK WALKO

STONEWALL PRESS
PAVING YOUR WAY TO SUCCESS

Published in the United States of America

ISBN: 978-1-64460-033-7 (*sc*)
          978-1-64460-032-0 (*e*)

Library of Congress Control Number: 2018961896

Stonewall Press books may be ordered through booksellers or by contacting:

Stonewall Press
4800 Hampden Lane, Suite 200
Bethesda, MD 20814 USA
www.stonewallpress.com
1-888-334-0980
orders@stonewallpress.com

1. Romance
2. Literature
18.12.14

Chapter 1

ROBBIE ROBERTS DRAGGED HIS suitcase into the room, turned to lock his hotel room door and immediately fell onto the bed.

"Holy shit!" he exclaimed aloud. "Did my dad just tell me that he was gay? Or bisexual?

What the hell is that? Bisexual?"

The conversation of the last hour had to be processed. Not only had his father told him that he was "bi" but he told him in front of Cee Jay as the two of them held hands. *"So, all along his buddy is really his lover,"* Robbie thought. *"And Cee Jay is Barbie's teacher! And Dad said that mom was at home telling her the same thing he and Cee Jay had just told me. What the fuck am I to make of this? He loves Mom, always did, but now he also loves the guy he loved even before I was born…What the hell!…And Mom knows all about it. And accepts it, for Christ's sake! I can just picture Barbie screaming as mom tells her that her senior year English teacher is Dad's lover.*

I thought something was up on Christmas when Dad suddenly said that he would go skiing with Cee Jay and me. I had asked Cee Jay to teach me how to ski and he agreed to take me to the Pocono Mountains during the holidays. Then Dad suddenly invites himself and decides that the three of us would stay in this hotel for three nights.

When we checked into the hotel, the three of us went to the same room, the one I thought Dad and I would share. Turns out this room only had one queen-size bed, so I thought it was Cee Jay's room. Then Dad dropped the bomb by giving me a key to my own room and telling me that this was his and Cee Jay's room. I guess he saw my immediate surprise, so he told me to sit down in the chair. He and Cee Jay sat on the edge of the bed. As Dad began to talk, I saw Cee Jay grab his hand and hold it as if he were giving him moral support.

Dad said, "I've been wanting to tell you and Barbie about Cee Jay and me for some time, and thought this get-away would be the best way to tell you. Cee Jay, your mom and I have discussed it and we all agree that you and your sister should know. You see, Robbie, Cee Jay and I knew one another in New York before you were born, but lost touch until this October when we met at the Mountain Ridge High Parents' Night. I loved Cee Jay when we knew one another in New York, but he was busy working on his doctorate and hardly gave me a second thought. When we met in October things were very different and we both are very much in love."

"And what about Mom?" I had asked.

"Your mother and I are still also very much in love. We always will be. We will not get a divorce, if that's what you're thinking. You see, Robbie, I am bi-sexual. That means that I like to have sex with men as well as women. Cee Jay, here—on the other hand—is homosexual or gay. He only has the capacity to love men, but we never had sex back then. Your Mom knew about my bi-sexuality before we were married; I had even discussed Cee Jay with her before you were born. The truth, Robbie, is that I had sex with quite a few men before you were born; but since then, I have been 100% faithful to your mother.

But now with Cee Jay reentering my life, I have renewed long suppressed feelings and needs."

"I bet this is all probably mind blowing to you," Cee Jay said entering the conversation for the first time. "Please understand that I will never come between your Dad and mother. I think it is fair to say that we love your old man here equally and that he loves us equally too. Your dad is one of those rare human beings who has great capacity for love and the ability to express that love regardless of traditional sex rolls. I really admire him for that ability and his honesty and courage to talk to you about this so openly."

"Your mother, Cee Jay, and I agree that you kids are mature enough to know the truth and that we should not have to hide our feelings for one another in front of you," Jamie said to his son. "Barbie may already be suspecting something between me and Cee Jay, so the three of us want to clear up any doubts about why Cee Jay and I are spending so much time together."

"I must admit that it is awkward for me to see your sister in my classroom after I have been with your father," Cee Jay said. "She is a very intelligent and insightful person. In less than two years you too will probably be in my class. I need to be honest and respectful of you both."

"Wow! I need time to take all of this in," Robbie had said getting up from the chair. "Thanks for confusing the hell out me." Jamie and Cee Jay both noted the sarcasm in Robbie's voice.

"Well, here's a first for you, Robbie: the key to your own hotel room. Think about what we told you, and we'll call you in about an hour to go for dinner. "

Back in his own room, Robbie really was confused. He didn't know whether he should cry, kiss his dad, hug his father's lover, or what? He knew that Cee Jay—or Charles John Seton, Ph.D.—had the reputation of being a good but hard—ass teacher at Mountain Ridge High. Barbie had told him she thought Cee Jay was the best teacher she had; and for her to say that, meant he really must have been super good. Robbie also liked to be around him when he came over to their house just to shoot hoops or talk. Whenever Cee Jay saw him in the halls at school, he always gave him a special 'Hi' or tap on the shoulder. Yeah, he was a good guy. But dad's bi-sexual lover? That would take some getting used to. He didn't even want to think of it. Two guys kissing, holding hands, jerking off together, or even fucking or sucking…Ugh!…Disgusting! Just for a moment he thought of his father and Cee Jay together in that queen-sized bed and wondered who did what to whom. He never thought of either man as anything but masculine. At school the guys who were called gay or faggot were all effeminate. His father certainly was not effeminate. Neither was Dr. Seton. So, how in hell could he be gay and his father "bi"?

About four years ago when his dad explained to Robbie about female parts and menstruating and how babies were conceived and born, he never said anything about being gay or "bi" then. He just talked about love and "doing what comes natural." He also lectured his son on being "safe" with girls and not over-doing masturbation. He was glad that his father spoke to him so openly about sex then; but he never mentioned anything about two guys doing it together. Those ugly details he was getting from his friends and other basketball players.

He was anxious to call his sister to see if she and his mom had their 'little talk' about dad and Cee Jay yet and get her view.

Chapter 2

THE HOTEL ROOM PHONE rang before Robbie could call Barbie.

"Hello, Robbie. This is dad. Are you about ready for dinner?"

"Yeah. I'm about as ready as I'll ever be today."

"Okay, We'll stop at your room on the second floor on our way down from the third. Hey, I just realized you must be directly under us. Your room number is 240. Ours is 340. "

"Oh, great. Now I have to put up with a creaking bed above me all night." Robbie said in his most sarcastic tone.

"Don't be such a smart ass," Jamie admonished and then quickly added: "See you in five, buddy."

Five minutes was not enough time to call home. He and his older sister would need more than five minutes to discuss the adults in their lives.

Robbie hated the thought of seeing Cee Jay and his dad; but since they skipped lunch, he was hungry, and he realized that sooner or later he would have to face the two "love birds," AKA sex deviants; so he was glad when they knocked a few minutes later. Robbie was startled to see the two men were well groomed, shaved, washed, and dressed in smart looking slacks and jackets and wearing almost matching ties. He had not changed clothes and was still in his jeans and plaid flannel shirt and white sneakers.

"Had I known we were modeling for GQ tonight," he said sarcastically. "I would have worn my tuxedo. This is a ski resort hotel, isn't it?"

"You might want to put on your denim jacket, Robbie. It's pretty cold out and we have to walk a short distance to get to the dining room," Cee Jay advised.

Robbie opened his suitcase and took out a jacket that he had packed. "mmm," Cee jay remarked eying Robbie from foot to head, "You know, in that jacket you almost look as sexy as your father."

"Yeah, sure. But remember, he's your boyfriend; not me. So don't try anything."

Robbie chuckled along with the two men as they left 240 and headed to the elevator.

The Manor's main dining room was rustic in an elegant way. The flooring was dark brown wood. One full side wall was red brick, opposite a full wall of glass sliding doors that in spring and summer would open to a spacious patio overlooking the current ski slopes. Dim lighting came from lanterns hanging from rafters. The ceiling was slanting upward, giving the room a barn-like feeling. On each of the wooden tables was a small votive candle and four checkered place mats. A young maître d' escorted the threesome to a table with a fine view of the slopes where a few stragglers were enjoying the last rays of light on the snow.

Robbie felt tense. The two adults felt awkward. All of them wished the feeling and the silence would end. They were glad that a waiter quickly came to their rescue. "My name is Daniel, and I'll be your waiter this evening. May I get you gentlemen a drink while you look at the menu?"

Cee Jay did the ordering. "Robbie, what will you have?"

"A vile of poison, please," was Robbie's sarcastic response. Daniel and the two men gave a shocked look, a slight gasp, and then a smile.

Chuckling, Cee Jay said, "You'll have to excuse the boy. He's had one of those days."

Robbie did not miss the emphasis Cee Jay gave to the word 'boy.' He knew exactly what Cee Jay intended by using it. "What 'the boy' meant to say was that he will have a coke. These two 'boys' will undoubtedly have the poison of their own choosing, which is to say, 'extra-dry martinis on the rocks, one with a lemon twist and one with olives.'" Cee Jay and Jamie looked at one another, then smiled and nodded to the waiter who grinned politely and quickly walked away.

"Someone knows us very well," Jamie said to Cee Jay.

"Indeed! But methinks the lady—er—the lad—doth protest too much, my lord."

"Sire, I do protest! I have indeed had one of those days. The news of the day is most disturbing."

"Very good, Robbie! Thou hast, indeed, heard the worst. But we mark with pleasure that thy humor is untainted. Thou art a true prince in that."

Jamie had no idea what the banter between his son and lover was about, but he was happy when Robbie, paused, smiled, and said to him. "Dad, I guess you are right. I have been a smart ass. I'm sorry, but I still haven't gotten over the story you guys gave me this afternoon."

"I know, son. It may take a long time for all of us to fully understand it; but Cee Jay and I will help you to realize the truth about us and that it is best that you know it. "Jamie paused. "And have heard it from us first," he added.

Daniel came back with their drinks. "One coke for the young man," he said placing it in front of Robbie. "And two vials of poison for the gentlemen. Now who gets the lemon?"

"If by 'lemon,' you mean 'the boy,' I do," Jamie said. "Because he is my loving son."

Daniel chuckled. "Oh, I'm really going to enjoy serving you guys. How long will you be staying at the Manor?"

"Three very long nights," Robbie offered.

"I guess you are here then for the special, two-day 'Learn to Ski' package."

"That's right," Jamie said. "My son has a lot to learn about skiing…and other things."

"I understand." Daniel winked. "Now, are you ready to order?"

The order was given and Daniel went into the kitchen. Cee Jay made a quick toast. "Here's to us and a great learn-to-ski experience." The other two said, "Here, here!" and the men began zipping their beverages.

During the meal, Cee Jay told Robbie that he had signed them both up for the beginner class in order to assist Robbie with getting adjusted to the skis and slopes and giving him moral support. Meanwhile, Jamie would immediately hit the intermediate slope and they would join him after the two-hour class was over for a hot cider on the patio before all of them took the pulley rope up the intermediate slope.

After Cee Jay signed the ticket for the meal and the men left the restaurant, they decided to walk around the resort gift shop, lobby, and game rooms where they played a game of pool. It was obvious that Robbie was the hustler who badly beat his father and Cee Jay and won three dollars from each of them. With his $6.00 in hand, Robbie then insisted the men go with him into the gift shop to get a cup he saw earlier with a picture of the resort painted on it.

While passing the indoor, heated swimming pool and hot tub, they decided that they would change into their swim suits and enjoy the pool before calling it a night.

An hour later Robbie was changed and ready to try out the pool. This time he was happy when the men knocked on his door.

Opening it, he was startled to see both men in bathing suits. True Robbie had seen his father in a bathing suit before, but never really gave it a thought. But it was Cee Jay that caught him a bit off guard. The usually casually—dressed but fashionable English teacher stood at his door in a red Speedo bathing suit. Robbie had never thought that he would be so muscular with a chest with just the right amount of hair to accentuate his well-defined abs. Just for a moment Robbie spied Cee Jay's also well-defined crotch. It was then that he realized that his father, who usually wore baggy surfers like his own, was now also wearing a black Speedo suit. As he grabbed for his room key on the dresser, the thought entered his mind that both men really had good-looking, well-toned bodies. Even he could see and admire this fact. *Is this what attracted gay—er—'bi' men to each other?* he thought.

They checked in with the pool receptionist, got their towels, and staked out three chaise lounges at the deep end. The pool was crowded with noisy little kids, splashing with plastic life preservers on their arms and parents gathering in groups to walk, talk, and cheer on their little charges. Robbie watched Cee Jay jump right in and begin to swim laps like an Olympian. His father followed but his stroke and breathing were way off; his abilities in the pool were about the same as his own. Robbie just sat at the edge watching the kids splashing. He wondered if any of those proud-looking daddies were also "bi." He remembered going to pools and lakes with his own proud dad and always liked the idea of splashing around with him. He loved those times. He loved his dad. But now his dad also loved Cee Jay. Robbie wondered if he could also ever love Cee Jay. He knew he could never ever, ever, ever love both of them in a physical way; but he did really love his father, and if his father loved Cee Jay the way he loved his Mom, maybe he could someday love Cee Jay too. *But definitely not today!* he thought. After a while both Jamie and Cee Jay swam over to him. They said that the pool was too crowded for any real swimming so they were going into the spa. Robbie declined their offer to join them opting instead to stay at the pool

When the men got out of the pool, Robbie jumped in, got himself wet over his head, swam a few laps but was frequently bumping into people, tried walking and jumping, and floating before just stopping at the shallow end before sitting on the edge. He was totally lost in thought when, seemingly, out of nowhere he heard someone call him.

"Hey, Roberts," the voice said. Robbie turned to his left and saw a young man approximately his own age who was also sitting on the edge about six feet away. Robbie did not recognize him, but returned the "Hi" anyway.

The stranger slide into the shallow water and walked over to Robbie. He jumped up to sit next to Robbie. "You are Robbie Roberts from Mountain Ridge High School, aren't you?"

"Yes," Robbie said with hesitation. "Do you go there too?"

"You betcha," the stranger said. I thought I recognized you. My name's Donavon Rice. Most kids just call me Don, however." He extended a hand and Robbie shook it. The boy's grip was firm and Robbie immediately sensed a genuine friendliness and bond. "I'm in a class with your sister Barbie. We have English together. Is she here with you?"

"No I'm here with my dad..." Robbie found it difficult to add to the sentence.

Donavon ended it for him. "And Dr. Seton. Yes, I saw the three of you in the dining room earlier. I'm here with my mother, step-father and little sister."

"Oh." He paused trying to say something next. Then it came to him. "Don Rice! You're the football player, right? I've seen your name a few times in the paper."

"That's right. I'm the quarterback. You're on the basketball team. I've seen you play quite a few times. You make the newspapers often too. You're good!"

"Not really as good as I'd like to be."

"Good enough to make it up to varsity as a sophomore; and now as a junior, you are very good." Donavon said quickly.

"I'm hoping we do better as a team this year," Jamie said in a shy manner, not seeming to be overly boastful, even though he knew he was good and grateful for the compliment.

There was a long pause as the two boys realized they didn't know what to say next, but also knew they didn't want to part so soon with the usual "see ya."

Donavon broke the silence. "Your dad and Dr. Seton seem to be good friends."

Robbie panicked. "What do you mean…they seem to be good friends?" he shot out.

"I'm sorry if I said something I shouldn't have, Robbie. I've seen the two of them together at football games as well as basketball games. And they both belong to the same fitness club I do. They're obviously together a lot, and they are here together now with you. So I was just making a statement that they seem to be good friends."

Robbie realized that it was he who had over-reacted to Don's statement. "Yeah, they are good friends. They have known one another since before I was born. They met in New York where Dr. Seton went to college."

During the silence that followed, Robbie thought that Don now knew just as much about the two friends as he did. He suddenly realized that he did not know where or how they met or even exactly when. Up to this point, Robbie had not thought about it. It didn't seem important before he was told that they were lovers. *Did they have sex together back in those days?*

The silence and Robbie's thoughts were interrupted by Don. "Well, here they come."

Robbie looked up to see Cee Jay and his father walking along the side of the pool in their direction. Cee Jay spoke first by greeting Don. "Well, hello, there Donavon. I'm glad to see you two met up." Turning to Jamie, he said, "Jamie, this is Donavon Rice." Jamie extended his hand and the two men shook.

"It's a pleasure to meet you, Mr. Roberts."

"Donavon is in the same class as Barbie," Cee Jay explained.

"Ah, good, good." He paused. "Don Rice? You were Mountain Ridge's quarterback this year. We went to most of the home games. You're a really good football player, Don. Your final pass in the game against Valley was spectacular. I'll never forget it." Jamie paused again. "Barbie never said that she had classes with you."

"Just Dr. Seton's," Don said. "And thanks for the compliment. I was just telling Robbie that I thought he had great potential for this year's basketball team."

"He sure does! Say, you'll have to come over to visit one of these days now that your season is over. We just came over to tell Robbie that we are going to turn in now. And he needs to be up and about for breakfast tomorrow by 8:00 so he can be ready for Ski School at 10:00."

Donavon smiled broadly. "That's great, Robbie. I had the class today and tomorrow I'm doing the intermediate slope. You'll like the instructors. Maybe I'll see you on the slope in the afternoon."

"It was good running into you, Donavon," Cee Jay said. "See you tomorrow."

This time it was Don who initiated the hand shake with Jamie and Cee Jay.

"You guys have a good night now. I'll call home later and tell Barbie we ran into you. Okay?"

"Sure. It was a pleasure meeting you, Mr. Roberts."

"Good night, dad. Night, Cee Jay."

As the men walked away, Donavon said, "You call Dr. Seton Cee Jay?"

"Yeah, but only when he's at our house. He prefers it that way."

"He's a good guy. And your dad is very friendly. You sure are lucky, Roberts, to have a father like him. I have to plead with my step-father to see even one game a year—usually on Thanksgiving Day. Your dad is always at the school; mine, almost never."

"Yeah, well, I guess I better be getting up to my room for the night too," Robbie said.

"I'm on the second floor in Tower Two," Donavon said. "How about you? Where's your room?"

"Same place, room 240."

"Cool. Let's go back together. I've had enough of this kiddy pool, anyway," Donovan said.

Chapter 3

Robbie woke up before the alarm went off. Realizing that today was the day he was going to learn to ski, he showered and dressed quickly. He was ready well before his 8:00am meeting with Cee Jay and his father for breakfast. Pulling open the drapes, he saw that it was a bright, sunny morning. He also saw that it had snowed more during the night because the trees were heavily laden and fresh snow covered the adjacent buildings. He already knew that his father and Cee Jay were proficient skiers, but he was glad that Cee Jay had told him that he would be with him in the beginners' class to give him as much help and support as he needed. *After all*, he thought, *it was he, Robbie, who asked Cee Jay to take him skiing in the first place*. Robbie was surprised how quickly the teacher agreed, but somewhat disappointed when his dad volunteered to tag along and extended the one day outing to three. He now realized that this was for the men to have the "little talk" with him and probably give mom enough time to do the same with Barbie. He had slept on the shocking revelation but still couldn't understand or believe it. He wondered if Barbie knew yet and what her reactions were.

Really, she has more to be concerned with, he thought. *After all, she sees him in class every day,* he thought.

And then there's Don Rice. He's in the same class with Barbie. What did he really think after seeing his teacher and 'friend' in tight-fitting, sexy swim suits? What did he really mean when he said 'They seem to be really close friends'? Did he suspect that the two guys were faggots? What if he starts blabbering about seeing them together to his friends at Mountain Ridge? Such a rumor could hurt the teacher. And if word got beyond school, it could hurt dad's business. Dad has a successful contracting and construction company. He's on the Chamber of Commerce and well-known in the county. And I know that in our fuckin' county, he would probably be tarred and feathered if this ever got out? What would his employees think about working for a gay or "bi" guy. Knowing some of them, he thought, *they would not know the difference. To them, both words mean 'sexual deviant.' And Mom? How is she going to face her friends and associates and those holier than thou hypercritics at Saint Anne's Roman Catholic Church? Dad, mom, and Cee Jay should have kept their dirty little secret to themselves. They didn't have to involve us in this mess. Hell, Barbie is getting out of dodge and going away to college in a few months. It's the rest of us, particularly me, who have to face the consequences of this. I was happier just knowing Cee Jay before without even thinking of what he and dad do in private.* As Robbie grabbed his room key off the dresser, he was determined to bring the subject up at breakfast.

Robbie was surprised to see how few people were in the dining hall. He looked around to see if Donavon and his family were there. *Thank God, they're not here,* he thought. They were seated at the same table as the night before, and Robbie was glad that Daniel would not be their waiter. He made a point of being politer and more mature to this one.

After placing their orders, it was Cee jay who broke the silence. "So, Robbie, did you and Donavon manage to have a nice time at the pool last night?"

"We talked for a while and then walked back to our rooms together. He's on the same floor as I am."

"Donavan is a fine young man. You know that he was our quarterback, but did you guys know that he is on the Cross Country team and just a few weeks ago got his Eagle Scout Badge?"

"Wow! That's something," Jamie said. "He seems like such a modest person. Not your typical high school jock type."

"Only a few people at school know about his award. I wouldn't have known about it if he didn't ask me to write a letter of recommendation for a scholarship to Rutgers. When I asked him to tell me a few things about himself that I might not know, he told me. I didn't even know he was a boy scout, let alone an Eagle Scout. With his sports record, Eagle Scout Badge, and excellent grade-point average, he deserves to get a scholarship."

"Robbie, I told your sister and mother that we ran into him at the pool last night. Your mom knows his mother. She told me that Mrs. Rice is a parishioner at Saint Anne's. She's also on the Altar Society and is the woman who sometimes reads the gospel at mass."

"Can we stop talking about Donavon," Robbie interjected, "and talk about why we are really here?"

"We're here because you wanted to learn to ski, I'm here to spend some quality time with you and Cee Jay, and for all of us to have a good time," Jamie quickly responded as the waiter brought their breakfast dishes.

"What Robbie wants to talk about is what we told him about ourselves yesterday afternoon," Cee Jay said in a rather admonishing tone to Jamie.

"Okay, Robbie, talk," Jamie responded.

"Thanks, Cee Jay. For starters, did mom tell Barbie about you two?"

"Yes."

"And...?"

"Well, when I spoke to Barbie, I asked her how she felt about Cee Jay and I being lovers. She told me that she wasn't too surprised because she kind of suspected something. She said that she wished it wasn't the case. She wished that we were just good friends; but if it were okay with mom, she would have to accept it also."

"Dad, did you guys consider the effects all of this may have beyond us?

"Do you mean the school and the community?" Cee Jay said.

"Yes." Robbie paused. "Of course!"

"Robbie, my family is the most important thing in my life. You, your mother and sister and now Cee Jay mean everything to me. I love you all dearly. You mean more to me than anything else in the world. Suppose some gossip mongering people started a dirty rumor about Cee Jay and I and you heard about it in the halls at school. How would that make you feel?

"Cee Jay and I are who we are, we can't deny it; we can't change it. We have to be ourselves. We are happy being who we are. We certainly can't hide the truth from my own family. We have to be honest with you. We felt it better that you hear it from us first. Sure, we considered the possibility of people voicing their prejudices and saying bad shit behind our backs. That's their fucking problem! And you shouldn't get it that way."

It was Cee Jay's turn to enter the conversation. "Robbie, we weighed all the pros and cons of telling you and Barbie. We couldn't continue if we weren't open and honest with you. As for others finding out and spreading gossip, your dad and I are not teenagers. We don't have the need to have an ostentatious display of affection in public like so many high school people. I assure you that we will never hold hands or kiss in public. Or, for that matter, even in your house. Both your dad and I are in the public eye, but we are also very private. You should never be embarrassed by us."

"But what if word does get out, and kids at school do start talking? How do I—and how do you—handle it?"

"That's an excellent question, Robbie," Jamie said. "So, let's start with you. We trust that you will never talk to anyone but Barbie about this. Not even your best friends in confidence. That said, we hope that you will handle gossip and rumor in a mature manner in your own way. We can't tell you exactly what to do or say, But we can offer you some advice."

"Like what kind of advice? Word is bound to get out now that Donavon Rice saw you two in sexy bathing suits last nights. He's a jock; and you know, Dr. S, how jocks talk. He even made a comment about you two to me last night."

"Really, what did he say?" Jamie asked.

"When you guys were walking away, he said that you two seemed like really good friends."

"Well, we really are good friends," Cee Jay said. "By the way, thanks for saying that we looked sexy in our bathing suits. How did you respond to Don's comment?"

"I asked him what he meant by it."

"And how did he answer?"

"He said that he had seen you together at games at school and at the fitness club in Sparta."

"mmm," Cee Jay reacted. "I don't remember ever seeing him there. But then again the place is usually crowded, and the only man I ever care to see there is your father," he said chuckling. "And we go there and leave in separate cars, often not at the same time; but not deliberately so." He paused for a moment. "But if I read Donavon Rice correctly, you don't have anything to worry about, Robbie. I do, however, question your reaction to his statement."

"What do you mean, Cee Jay?"

"Well, the first bit of advice your dad and I can give you is to never over-react. I know you are a sensitive person, and that is good; but yesterday you were understandably emotional and probably did over-react by asking him what he meant. He could have been making a simple and true comment that we were good friends. By reacting as you did, someone else may have interpreted your question negatively. Do you see what I'm getting at?"

"Yes, I do," Robbie said after a short, thoughtful pause. "I may have even been a little rude to Don."

"Good boy for recognizing that." Cee Jay smiled.

"And for a second bit of advice," Jamie said, "never be belligerent or defensive. That only stirs people up more."

"That's right," Cee Jay added. "One of your sarcastic, but pointed, humorous lines can go farther to defuse a situation than to deny it."

"Okay, guys. Enough of the lecturing for the morning," Jamie said. "Let's get out and do some skiing and have some fun."

Cee Jay signed the check and the men went back to their rooms to get ready for the slopes. He told Robbie to meet them at the ski rental shop at 9:30.

Robbie was in an enthusiastic and cheerful mood at 9:30 when he met the men. "Let's do this!" he excitedly greeted them.

All three had to be fitted out with shoes and skis. They stowed their own shoes and Cee Jay signed for their rentals. Robbie and Cee Jay headed to the instructional area. Jamie told them he would meet them on the deck after their class was over around noon. They would have a beverage and snack before spending the rest of the day on the mountain.

Robbie's ski instructor was a young girl not much older than Barbie. He thought she was very pretty and very patient with her diversified twenty students who seemed to range in age from seven to Cee Jay, who obviously was the oldest but best "beginner." Carol, the instructor, caught on quickly that Cee Jay was there only to help awkward Robbie. At one point, she even said, "Your son seems to be catching on quickly." The remark made Robbie smile because in a way he did feel like Cee Jay's 'son.' Rather than correcting her, Cee Jay said, "He's a great athlete." That caused Robbie to beam with pride and enhance his admiration for his dad's lover. Just for a moment he thought to himself: *No wonder my dad loves this man.*

The ski student did not realized how tiring learning the sport could be. After an hour of falling and getting up, learning to walk by pushing yourself without lifting your feet, and finally getting the knack of stopping, he was sweating inside his parka, even though he knew it was below freezing. He noticed that a few students, including the seven-year old little girl, left the group and were slowly trying to get back to the rental shop. Robbie refused to admit to Cee Jay that he wanted to rest for a while.

During the second hour of the class., each student had to individually walk up the slope, turn around, and ski back down turning left and right before stopping directly in front of the instructor. Carol then gave each of them a critique on what he or she did right. The other students were actually encouraged to cheer during each student's performance. Cee Jay, being the good sport he was, began showing off on his way down and rather than stopping in front of Carol, deliberately fell in front of her and pleaded with Robbie to help him get up.

At noon, when the class ended, everyone clapped for Carol and said that she was a wonderful instructor. Even Cee Jay told her that he learned a "few new things" from her and that he would be putting them into practice on the upper slopes later in the day. Shaking his hand, Carol said, "Just make sure your son doesn't get over-confident and try stuff he's not ready for. Many teenagers start showing off and have accidents." Again, either Cee Jay didn't hear or ignored her use of the word "son" and merely replied, "Don't worry, I'll keep him in check."

On the way back to the deck, they stopped to take off their skis and secure them on racks. Robbie told Cee Jay that he was up for a cheeseburger, fries, and a hot chocolate but was anxious to put his lesson into practice later. As they walked up the few steps to the deck, Cee Jay told him to grab a table and three chairs and look for Jamie while he headed to the line at the concession for their food and beverages.

Robbie didn't have to try very hard to find both a table and his father. "Hey, Roberts, Over here!" he heard someone call. That 'someone' was Donavon Rice, and sitting with him at a large picnic table was Jamie. *I can't believe this*, Robbie thought as he was compelled to walk in their direction.

"Hey, guys. I'm glad you got a table. Dr. S, is over at the concession getting some food. I see you already were there."

"Yeah, we got here a few minutes ago before the classes ended. So tell us, Robbie, how was your class? Are you ready for the intermediate slopes this afternoon?" Donavon asked.

"Yeah, the instructor was awesome. I'm psyched!."

"That's great to hear," Jamie said. "Don and I were just talking about you two going on the intermediate this afternoon while Cee Jay and I take to the half-expert slope."

"Well, I promised Cee Jay I'd be with him."

"Ah, let the older guys be by themselves, Robbie. I'm sure Dr. Seton would prefer to ski with your dad; and to be honest, I would really like to ski with a pal. I've been on the intermediate all morning, so I can help you if you have any problems. We can really have a blast together."

Robbie looked at his father. Jamie said, "I agree with Don, but let's see what Cee Jay thinks before we decide."

"Awesome!" Don exclaimed. "So, was your instructor the cute blonde, Carol?"

Before Robbie could respond, Cee Jay appeared with a tray containing Robbie's hamburger, fries, and hot chocolate and a hot cider and soft pretzel for himself. "Well, if it isn't the

Mountain Ridge gang. Amazing what they allow at the Manor Ski Resort these days," he jokingly said.

"I can see you have been hanging around my sarcastic son too long, Dr. Seton. His attitude and remarks are beginning to rub off on you."

"Hello, Dr. Seton. Robbie was just telling us how he aced Carol's class this morning. Is that true? Do you think he's ready for the intermediate slope this afternoon?"

"No question about it. That pretty blonde really motivated both of us."

"Cee Jay, Don was just asking if he and Robbie could do more practicing together on the intermediate hill while you and I go on the big boys' chair. What do you think?"

"I think that's a great idea!" Cee Jay explained. "As long as they stay together and don't try any crazy stuff. Don has a little more experience to help, and the peer pressure and comradery would be good for both of them. And we older guys can have some comradery of our own."

Why he emphasized the word 'comradery' left Robbie speechless. *How gay is that?* Robbie thought. *Comradery! And now I have to listen to this jock football player, super trooper Boy Scout, and brainy senior lord over me all afternoon. What the hell are dad and Cee Jay doing?*

Cee Jay and Jamie decided they would first rest a bit and wash up before going back on the slopes. It was Donavon who suggested that they do the same; Don said that he would knock on '240' in an hour and they would go together to get their skis and go up the intermediate slope on the chair together.

Robbie was apprehensive about all of this, but went along with the plan to please his dad and Cee Jay. But it was really Donavon who laid the matter to rest, when in the elevator he confessed, "I'm really glad we can spend the afternoon together, Robbie. I've been pretty lonely being here just with my step dad, mom, and little step sister. They are content to sit in the game room and play cards. My step father only needs a can of beer to keep him company. Evie, my little step sister actually left the class we were in with Carol before it was over. She said skiing was boring. God, you don't know how lucky you are to have a family like yours."

Later, on their way to the intermediate chair lift, all Robbie could think of was why Donavon had told him how lucky he was to have 'a family like yours.' *If he only knew how crazy my family really is,* he thought, *he would never say that. I bet his beer guzzling, couch-potato step-dad is not gay...Or 'bi'. Or did Don just say that because he suspected something about Cee Jay and dad and wanted me to talk about them?*

When the chair lift started, Robbie realized for the first time how heavy his boot and skis were as his feet dangled off the ground. He turned to Don and was about to tell him when he realized that the senior boy was already looking directly at him with a pleasant smile. Robbie was caught off guard and couldn't speak. Sitting so close now, he suddenly realized how good-looking Donavon was. This was something he had never thought of before. He knew that Don had piercing blue eyes, but now with sun goggles and a light 'five o'clock' he resembled one of those GQ models he had seen in a ski magazine in his room. Don had pulled down the hood on his parka, and the sun light shining on his thick, light brown hair created an aura around his clear, clean face. Robbie was conscious of his own pimply face. Jamie had told him that he too had pimples as a teen and that they would go away. Robbie wondered if Don every had pimples.

When they got off the chair, Don led Robbie to a spot where they stood almost by themselves against the sky.

"Beautiful, isn't it," Don said finally.

Taking in the panoramic view of sky, pine trees, and the lodge below them, Robbie was thrilled and filled with a sense of pride. Here he was on top of the intermediate slope already with his school's quarterback. This senior Adonis who just an hour ago implied he was his 'pal.'

Don pulled his hood back over his head. "Okay, Roberts. Let's ski," he practically shouted. "I'll stay by your side this time down," he added before pushing off.

Robbie followed. He kept an eye for any moguls, ice patches and big depressions in the hill. He was remembering all that Carol and Cee Jay had told him as he picked up speed on the soft powder. He was aware that every so often Don would look over at him to make sure he was properly positioned with the hill and had his knees bent forward the right way. Robbie saw how Don held his poles and adjusted his own hold similarly. Robbie was a bit nervous having Don watch him so closely, but it did make him feel safer knowing that he was so close. He also didn't want to make a fool of himself in front of this senior who was willing to be a 'pal' to a pimply-faced junior, even if it was only for a day. He didn't relish the ridicule that Donavon and his jock friends might make if he skied like a little kid or— worse—like a girl.

All too soon they reached the bottom of the slope and stopped perfectly.

"Wow! That was awesome!" Robbie said turning to Don. Let's go up again."

"Sure, you're up to it, Roberts?"

On the lift for the second time, Don suggested that they try lengthening their descent by zigzagging to the left and right more than they had during the first run. Robbie's consent was answered with a punch on his arm by the senior. As they positioned themselves for the run, Don told Robbie to relax and enjoy the ride down-hill. He told him to take the turns slowly and that he would stay close to him. The second run was all pleasure as Robbie's confidence was increased. By the time they reached the bottom, both boys realized their faces were icy cold and turning pink and their noses were running. Their mutual accomplishment was greeted by a bear hug equal to any that they had received on the basketball court or football field, but Robbie suddenly felt awkward hugging Don this way. Sure it was natural for Don to initiate a bear hug, but this seemed different for some reason. They weren't on a team. Don was a handsome senior; he was a mere junior. They hadn't scored. But Robbie really liked having Don's arms around him. This hug seemed to send a thrill through him that Robbie had never experienced before. As the two boys pulled apart, Robbie had the feeling that Don realized this too.

On the chair lift for the third time that afternoon, rather than just letting his skis hang down, Robbie deliberately tapped Don's ski with his. Don responded by immediately crossing his leg over Robbie's. Their two legs touched. Neither boy moved. Both experienced a new, thrilling sensation that neither could deny and neither were in a hurry to end as the chair neared the jumping off point.

"Hey," Robbie said at last. "This time I'll race you to the bottom. First one down has to treat the loser to a hot chocolate."

"No!" was Don's curt reply.

"Why not? Afraid the big Mountain Ridge jock may lose?"

"No! Because the Mountain Ridge senior varsity 'athlete' knows he would win. And remember, I promised your dad and Dr. Seton that we would play safe and not try any crazy stuff."

"Yeah, Carol warned me about that too," Robbie said sheepishly.

"Besides," Don commented. "I want to make sure the new varsity man on our basketball team gets home in one piece."

"Thanks for caring, Don."

"That's what friends are for!" Don shouted back as he started down the slope.

Robbie lingered in thought. *So that's what we are now: friends. I wonder how long that will last back at Mountain Ridge High?*

This time Robbie would ski down the slope on his own. He knew that Don was way ahead of him and that he could not catch up, so he took his time to enjoy the full experience. He was still cautious but enjoyed the freedom of being on his own. He was happy that his new 'friend' had confidence in his ability and no longer had to watch over him.

As he approached the bottom, Robbie saw Don looking up and waiting for him. He was glad his new friend was there.

"How about that hot chocolate break now?" Robbie asked.

"You betcha! Dutch treat, though. Okay"

While they waited at the concession, Robbie started a conversation about the Boy Scouts. "Cee Jay told my dad and me that you were recently awarded an Eagle Scout Badge."

"Yes, about two weeks ago. It's a big deal to some. Yeah, the mayor was at the ceremony. So was our congressman, the pastor of Saint Anne's, and a lot of Scout leaders. I even had my picture in the newspaper." Donavon said this in a matter of fact way. There was no boastfulness in his voice.

"Wow! That's awesome!" Robbie said. "How come I never heard anyone from school talking about it?"

"Probably because I never invited anyone. Other than Dr. S and now you, I haven't mentioned it to anyone. Of course, the four guys from my team who helped me knew about it, but didn't bother to go to the ceremony."

"I would have been there if I knew you then."

"Yeah, sure. Roberts, you're full of shit." He rubbed his hand over Robbie's head in a fun gesture. "Three weeks ago, you didn't even know I existed."

"Well, I'm glad to know you now, Donavon Rice."

"Same here, Robert Roberts. 'Robert Roberts.' That's a crazy name to give a kid. I guess you will go by 'Robbie' until you're an old man. Was your dad getting back at the person who named him 'Jamie' or is 'Jamie just a nick name for 'James.'

"No, it's not a name for James. I can't tell you what his name really is."

"Why not?"

"Because you'd laugh and then start calling him by his real name. Then he'd hate both of us. Me, for telling you and you for using it. He hates his given name."

"Ah, come on Roberts. You can tell me. I swear I'll never tell anyone."

"Well, if you must know, it's 'Jeremiah.' So now you know, and I'll kill you if you ever mention it to anyone."

Donavon burst out laughing. 'j-e-r-e-m-i-a-h' he stretched the name out long. "Yeah, your father is no Jeremiah, so I guess it will always be Jamie."

Robbie laughed too, but immediately he was telling too much about his father. He suddenly felt uncomfortable telling family secrets. He feared what secrets he might share next with his "new friend." *I should be more cautious,"* he thought. He wondered how Cee Jay would take this disclosure. *Even Cee Jay might not know dad's real name.*

The boys made two more runs on the slope before calling it a day. Donavon suggested that they get together after dinner to shoot billiards and maybe go into the hot tub to relax after skiing all day. Robbie agreed that Don should knock on the door of room 240 at eight o'clock.

Meanwhile, in room 340 there were two other males with some plans of their own.

Chapter 4

CEE JAY FELL INTO the chair in room 340 and turned on the television with the remote that he found on the seat. Jamie started to undress the minute they came into the room.

"A nice hot shower will feel wonderful after that workout on the slopes," Jamie said.

"Save some hot water for me," Cee Jay responded after watching his lover get down to his briefs. He was more intent on Jamie than the news.

"How about we take a shower together," Jamie said putting his arms around Cee Jay's neck and kissing him lightly on the cheek.

Cee Jay immediately noticed Jamie's erect cock protruding from his briefs and teasingly brushed it aside. In his best southern-belle accent he said, "Well, ma dear Mista Roberts, I do declare. You do seem to have a problem with that litta thing thar. Twice in one day! You'll wear little ole me out with your lasciviousness."

Jamie loved this banter that his lover could come up with at times. He started to unbutton Cee Jay's plaid flannel shirt.

"Why Mister Seton," he said in his General Sanders deepest voice, "you know those vapors will do your little heart a world of good. They're just what the doctor ordered."

"mmm. And just what this doctor wants," Cee Jay grabbed Jamie's fully erect cock again.

"Now you get yourself into that shooow-weer and make sure the water's good and hot for little ole me, ya hear. I do like it hot, you know."

Jamie turned around and gave his ass a little twist as he walked to the bathroom.

When Cee Jay pulled the shower curtain open, he found Jamie standing under the water facing him. Jamie had a grin on his face a mile wide.

Cee Jay took him in his arms and passionately kissed him on the lips. His tongue was met by Jamie's who wrapped his arms around Cee Jay's back. He started moving his hand around Cee Jay's shoulders. Slowly he moved his hands around and up and down until he gently began to play with Cee Jay's ass. Cee Jay moaned and pulled his lover closer to himself. He felt his hard cock connect with his own. He grabbed both cocks in his hand and gently tugged on both as he continued to circle Jamie's lips with his tongue. Jamie fell to his knees and put his mouth on his lover's engorged member. He looked up to see Cee Jay staring down at him. The hot water was dripping on his head as Jamie began in earnest to pleasure his man. Cee Jay felt himself close to orgasm, but not wanting to come so quickly, pulled Jamie up to him. Their mouths met in a long embrace.

Cee jay began to play with Jamie's ass again. This time it was he who went down on his knees. He turned Jamie around to get a better look at his ass. He spread Jamie's cheeks and put his finger and then two into the hole. He moved them around before replacing his fingers with his tongue. Jamie yelled out in pleasure. Cee Jay dug deeper into the crack and then moved his entire face into Jamie's ass. Slowly, he moved his tongue from the base of his spine to Jamie's perineum. He crawled under Jamie to grab his balls in his mouth. He then licked at each ball lovingly and then together. Jamie pulled away to turn facing him. Cee Jay put his hands on Jamie's legs. As he moved his hands around Jamie's strong muscled legs, he rubbed Jamie's cock over his face. He slid his tongue up and down Jamie's shaft and teased his pee slit before putting the throbbing cock in his mouth.

He loved the taste of Jamie's precum and wanted to take it all, but Cee Jay wanted to come in Jamie's ass first, so he pulled out and stood up and gently turned Jamie around.

"Fuck me," Jamie said as he turned to kiss Cee Jay one more time before bending his back slightly so his ass would be better lined up with Cee Jay's cock. Cee Jay took no time slowly at first penetrating Jamie' tight hole and then sliding his dick in more when he knew Jamie was ready to accept all of it. "Oh, yes, yes!' Jamie breathed. "Give it to me, lover. Give me that big, thick cock of yours. Shove it all the way in. You know I love it."

Cee Jay held onto Jamie's body with one hand and reached around to grab his erection with the other. After knowing that his cock was massaging Jamie's prostrate, he took his hand off his penis. Experience taught him that in this position Jamie would climax quickly, and Cee Jay wanted him to come in his mouth, not in his hand. He yearned for Jamie's cum in his throat as much as Jamie wanted to feel him come in his ass.

Playing the dominant role always excited Cee Jay. He loved fucking Jamie's cute, little bubble ass and tight hole. Being inside Jamie made him feel whole. Natural. Manly. "This is the way men should do it," he had once said to Jamie. And he knew that more than anything else they might do sexually, Jamie loved being penetrated by a man. This was something that no woman could give him. The fact that Jamie also totally loved him made their sex all the more meaningful. When Cee

Jay felt himself reaching climax, he began pounding on Jamie's ass. Jamie became limp with pleasure. Cee Jay exploded inside Jamie and shouted Jamie's name as he felt his own release.

Jamie stood erect and Cee Jay wrapped his arms around him from the back. He gently kissed the back of his lover's neck and shoulders. Eventually and slowly, he removed his dick. There had been an earlier discussion about condoms, but both men preferred bare backing. Together they had been tested at the Newton clinic and now felt completely confident.

Cee Jay turned the shower faucet off. "Now, it's your turn to get your rocks off, Mister Roberts." He knelt down and immediately started jerking and sucking Jamie's still enlarged cock. Jamie came quickly and Cee Jay swallowed all of his load. Some of his semen was still on Cee Jay's lips and around his mouth when Jamie pulled him up and they kissed. "mmm. I like your lip balm," Jamie joked as he turned the shower on again to wash up.

Still with the glow of their love making, they dried one another and started to get dressed for dinner in fresh clothes. They told Robbie that they would knock on his door at 6:00.

"I've been wanting to ask you something."

"Yes," Cee Jay questioningly responded. "What about?"

"Well, this morning you said that if you read Donavon Rice correctly, he would never say anything about us." Jamie emphasized the word 'read.' "Were you implying that you thought Donavon might be gay?"

"Yes, I did mean it that way."

"Why?"

"Oh, just let's say my gaydar seldom lets me down."

"Yes, but what is it about him that sets your bells off?"

"I really can't put an exact finger on it, Jamie. It's just a thought and probably way too soon for any real judgment. Actually, I think he is probably still very much a virgin and doesn't know what he likes at this point."

"Yes, like my son. Cee Jay, the kid is already seventeen and a junior in high school; and, as far as I can see, he doesn't even care about girls…Or boys, either!…All Robbie is interested in seems to be model airplanes and basketball. When I gave him the old 'birds and bees' talk a few years ago, he just thanked me for it. Since then, notta. Nothing! I sometimes wonder if he even jerks off."

"How would you feel if someday he told you that he was gay?"

"I wouldn't care if he were straight or gay. His mother would prefer him to be straight so she can have grandchildren someday, but probably wouldn't really care. We have Barbie for the grandkids. Like me, I guess she would just want him to be happy either way."

"What if he turns out to be bisexual, like you, Jamie?"

"I wouldn't want him to go through all the trouble I had. You know I was sucking guys off before I was in my teens and fucking broads before I was Robbie's age. Thank God I met the perfect girl and was married and became a father for the first time while I was only seventeen. You know what I was doing hanging out in gay bars in New York. I had some very hard times, and I don't want that kind of life for my son, Cee Jay."

"I'm sure Robbie will turn out to be a great young man, Jamie. You and his mom will be proud of him no matter what. Just let him grow up and discover love at his own pace. You should be happy right now that all he is interested in is basketball and model airplanes.

"Come on now. We don't want the future pilot to be starving. It's past 6:00, and he's probably thinking that we're having wild, passionate sex up here," Cee Jay said while leading Jamie out of room 340.

Chapter 5

ROBBIE SEEMED LESS TROUBLED by their disclosure than he had been. As a result, their dinner conversation had been light. Robbie told the men about how he had improved gradually on the slope. He told them that he enjoyed getting to know Donavon better, and that they had planned to get together later that night to shoot pool. Jamie claimed to be a better skier than Cee Jay which resulted in much back and forth wise-cracking between the men, particularly when Robbie took Cee Jay's position.

While they were waiting for their dessert, Donavon had suddenly appeared at their table. "I just came over to say goodbye," he said. "My step-dad has to work tomorrow, so we will be leaving very early. "

"That's too bad, Don. Robbie was just telling us how he enjoyed skiing with you this afternoon." Jamie stood up and shook Don's hand. "It was good meeting you. "

"Same here, Mr. Roberts. Perhaps I'll see you and Dr. Seton at some home basketball games."

Cee Jay also now stood and shook his hand. "Well, like it or not, you will see me Monday morning in English class."

"In deed you will, sir." He smiled broadly and looking directly at Robbie asked, "Are we still on for meeting in the game room at eight, Robbie?"

"Sure, I'm looking forward to beating you in a game of pool."

"Be careful, Don. Robbie's a real hustler. He swindled his dad and me out of six bucks last night. "

"Don't worry, Dr. Seton. I'll keep my eyes on him so he better not pull anything. But I don't bet anyway. Have a good night, gentlemen, Bye."

"That was very nice of him to come over and say goodbye," Jamie said. "I'm sorry that we never got to meet his mother and father."

Daniel, the waiter, came with their desserts. After they left the dining room, the men told Robbie that they were going to have a drink and enjoy the entertainment in the lounge for a while before going to their room for the night. They arranged to meet the next morning and then to spend the day on the slopes.

Robbie was not sure whether Don was to knock on 240 at eight o'clock or if they were to meet in the game room, so he waited until 8:10; and when Don did not knock on his door, he went to hopefully meet him in the game room.

Donavon was waiting for him at one of the four pool tables. "I was beginning to think maybe you wouldn't come," he said.

The young men played two games. Try as hard as he could, Donavon was no match for Robbie who won both games quickly. "You have as good an eye for billiards as you do for the hoops," Don conceited. "Say, why don't we get into our swim suits now and hit the pool and spa for a while?" he suggested.

"That was the plan," Robbie said. "So, let's do it."

They changed in their rooms and just as Robbie was ready, Donavon knocked on his door. The pool was nearly empty at this time of evening. "All the little kids must be in bed,"

Don said. "Now we can really swim without bumping into anyone." He jumped into the deep end without waiting for Robbie.

Robbie stood watching Donavon swim two complete laps. He admired the way Don swam so effortlessly. His strokes and breathing were perfectly timed as he seemed to slither through the water. He knew that Don was a much better swimmer. Don stopped in front of him. Looking up, he shook the water from his hair and smiled at Robbie. "Aren't you coming in?"

"I...I was just watching you. How did you learn to swim so well?"

"At Boy Scout camp every year. Last year I got an award for speed. This summer, I'll be working there as a life guard and swim instructor."

Robbie jumped into the pool next to Don. When he came to the surface, he said, "I wish I could swim as well as you."

"Stick with me, kid, and maybe you will." Saying that he began to swim to the other end.

Yeah, Robbie thought. *Stick with him! Next week in school he'll pretend he never knew me. I'm just company for him for today. But it would be nice if we could ...be friends.*

They swam several laps before getting out of the pool and going to the hot tub. "I'll set the timer for fifteen minutes," Don said. "You should never stay in longer than that." Robbie got into the tub just as the jet streams started; Don waited to make sure that the timer and temperature set were proper before walking down the few steps into the spa.

For the second time that day Robbie found himself thinking of how good-looking Donavon was. *Real GQ material*, he thought again. He noticed Don's smooth shaven, six-pack abs, his well-developed nipples. His arm muscles were twice as big as his own. For the first time, he was aware that Don's wet bathing suit clung to his body. He felt embarrassed by his own realization that the suit outlined Don's manhood. For a second he wondered if Don was wearing a jock strap.

"Hot enough for you, Roberts? It's set for 103. After fifteen minutes of this, you'll sleep like a baby tonight." He paused, taking the tile bench opposite Robbie. "I wish I could be on the slope with you tomorrow."

That last sentence was said with such conviction, Robbie was stunned. After a few seconds, he responding. "Yeah, me to."

Robbie felt awkward. He looked at Don, who had closed his eyes and was thinking of how refreshing the hot water was. Eventually, Robbie broke the silence. "Don, what was your Eagle Scout project? Don't you have to complete some big project to get that award?"

"Yes. My project was not earth shaking, but it did take me about two years to complete. If I could do it over, I would have chosen a much simpler project. At first I thought it would be easy but soon found out it was complicated."

"Why was that?"

"Well, have you seen the bus stop benches and shelters at the new Walmart on route 23 or the one in front of the Rosemont Nursing Home or the one on Elliot Street across from Mountain Ridge?"

"Yeah, I know about the one across from the high school. It was just built this past fall."

"Yes, all three were my Eagle badge project. I had to think of something that would help the community, get a group to help me, and then to actually built them. The hardest part was raising the money to buy the materials. Each of those shelters cost about $300 dollars just for the materials. Labor costs weren't even considered. My friends and team mates had to have car washes, donations from differed businesses, and actual door-to-door canvassing for donations. Then I had to design them and present my plans to the town council before they issued the permits. The Council was very encouraging and even made some good suggestions. Once we had the money and the permits, the actual building was kind of fun and didn't take long."

"Wow. That's awesome! I had no idea who put up the shelter at the Elliot Street bus stop. I thought the city built it or the school board."

"No, it was just me and my buds. But I got all the credit for it. And the Eagle badge," Don added. "It also helped me to decide what my major should be in college."

"Really? Do they have a major in bus stop shelter building?"

"No," Don said, laughing at Robbie's comment. "But I did like many of the aspects of my project and I'd like to make a career out of one or two of them or combine some of them in multiple majors in college. You can do that at Rutgers."

"Like what?"

"I've been thinking about engineering and/or architecture for several years. Actually, designing those shelters was fun. I like to make something that people can use or live in.

By working on my project, I also developed a stronger interest in law and politics. So right now, I'm thinking of law and architecture. And there's also business."

"Awesome!" Robbie exclaimed. "You can design the buildings. My dad can build them and my mom can handle the business end. My mom is working to get a Master of Business Administration degree. She's been managing dad's business for years."

"I'll have to keep all of that in mind," Don said chuckling. "And what about you, Robbie? What would you like to be besides being a player for the Nets, or being a champion skier, or learning to be an Olympic swimmer?"

Just then the hot water jets stopped. "Oh, I'd like to be an aeronautical engineer and pilot," Robbie said.

"Good for you, Roberts. Just don't become as crazy as Howard Hughes." Don led the two out of the spa. As he went up the steps, Robbie noticed that Don's suit was also clinking to his ass and accentuated his crack.

Neither boy spoke on their way to the second floor. In front of room 240 Don said, "Well, I guess this is it, Roberts." Before

Robbie could do or say anything, Don grabbed him in a bear hug. The moment caught Robbie off guard as he felt Don's almost naked hot body against his. Don padded his young friend's back. "I'm glad I finally got to meet you, Roberts. I've wanted to for some time, you know." He hesitated. "You take care now. Don't do anything stupid on the slopes tomorrow. I'll see you around."

"Yeah, see ya," he said putting his key in the door.

Very softly, walking down the hall to his own room, Donavon said, "Gaa' night, buddy."

Robbie didn't fully realize that he had an erection until he turned on the room light. He touched his wet bathing and a shot of pleasure swarmed over him. He could not understand fully what brought it on. Usually, when he got a hard-on, it was because he was feeling horny. Was this because of Donavon? Did Don make him horny? No, that would be crazy. Then he thought of Don's strange bear hug, how good his body felt next to his own. He suddenly remembered Don rubbing his back and how good that felt. His erection grew tighter and he rubbed it again. *I have to get out of this bathing suit and take a shower*, he thought. He also needed to get rid of the feeling in his crotch; he had to get rid of any thought of Don in a sexual way. *Oh, my God*, he thought, *"was I hard when Don was hugging me? What if Don felt it?*

If Don thought I had the hots for him and blabbed about it to his jock buddies, I'd be doomed.

He practically tore off the wet suit and jumped in the shower. The water was cold at first, but it did the job of calming down his emotions and stop him from concentrating on Don

When he lathered, he deliberately avoided touching his penis. He didn't want to jerk off thinking of Don.

He managed to dry off and crawl into bed without getting another erection. In the dark room, with the warmth of the blanket surrounding his body, however, the thought of Donavon's arms encircling him brought on an involuntary feeling in his cock. He put his hand down to check. As he did so, he realized that he was fully hard again. He couldn't avoid the wonderful feeling it gave him, and he couldn't stop thinking of Donavon Rice. He imagined it was not his own hand, but Don's messaging his cock.

Chapter 6

ROBBIE HAD SLEPT VERY well. He remembered Donavon had said that after skiing and the hot tub he would sleep like a baby. Well, he certainly had; but he wondered if the reason he fell asleep so quickly and so soundly wasn't because he had jerked off. How could he possibly have thought of Donavon while jerking off? In the past, he never thought of anyone in particular. He also realized that no image of a girl had ever given him the same feeling. He just liked the feeling. Getting out of bed, he vowed to stop thinking of Donavon Rice. To himself, he said, *Only a fag would think about another guy while jerking off, and I ain't no fag!*

But the reality of his father and Cee Jay was there. That was real! He had to dress quickly before the men would be knocking on his door to go for breakfast.

In the dining room Jamie was particularly interested in knowing how Robbie enjoyed his evening with Donavon, a topic that Robbie would have preferred not to discuss, or even think about

"I beat him in two games of pool and then we went swimming for a while." He paused. "Oh, and then we went in the spa."

Sensing that Robbie was not going to add any details, Cee Jay, said, "Your dad and I had a lot of fun in the ratskeller last night. Your dad entertained the whole bar. I didn't know he was such a good singer."

"They had karaoke last night, and this guy dared me to get up and sing; so I entertained the troops for a while."

"He and mom sing around the house once in a while. It's embarrassing for Barbie and me."

"You shouldn't be embarrassed, Robbie. He sings very well. I know he chose to sing *First Time Ever I Saw Your Face* for me, but the audience loved it as much as I did and kept asking him to sing more. You should have seen him dancing around the floor to a few country tunes. His moves were terrific."

"Yeah, I bet. How many martinis did he have?" Robbie sarcastically asked.

"I can't get any respect from this guy," Jamie said, trying to give his best Rodney Dangerfield impression.

Robbie smirked.

The conversation turned to making plans for a day on the ski slopes.

Later, all three went up the intermediate slope. Cee Jay was on a chair by himself while Jamie and Robbie rode together in front. Robbie liked being with his dad like this, but he would have preferred to be next to Donavon. He felt sorry for Don whose step-father seemed so distant. "You know, dad, Don told me that he and his step-father never do anything together. I'm so glad that you and me are together."

"I know, son. And I'm happy being here with you. Our relationship will always be great for both of us," he smiled and gave Robbie a shoulder tap.

"In spite of Cee Jay," he said.

"I'm happy to hear you say that, Robbie. I do love Cee Jay, but no one will come between you and me."

"Okay," Robbie said. "Now let's do some serious skiing."

The three-some made four runs on the intermediate slope. They enjoyed crisscrossing in front of one another and slowing down to let one of them pass, but they always arrived at the same spot at the bottom so that they could go back on the chairs together. On the second run, Robbie lost his balance and fell, but Cee Jay and Jamie were immediately there to help him and give new advice.

After stopping on the deck for cider and soft pretzels, Jamie suggested that they go on the advanced-level slope. "What do you say, Robbie, are you ready to join us big boys?"

"Sure thing!" Robbie said enthusiastically. "As long as you guys stay close to me. He paused. "At least at first," he added."

"Good boy! Cee Jay chimed in. "We'll be close!"

Cee Jay's last sentence: 'We'll be close' had special meaning for Jamie. Robbie sensed it also.

As they went down the mountain for the last time, the sun was rapidly setting into an orange ski. Streaks of red accented the crescent moon which was beginning to appear above the lodge. The atmosphere had the feeling of an impending blizzard. All admitted they were cold and ready for a hot shower followed by a leisurely dinner.

"So, gentlemen, how are my favorite skiers this evening?" Daniel said approaching their table. "I don't see any crutches, so that's a good sign." Directly to Robbie, he asked, "Was this your first time skiing, young man?"

"Yes, and I did quite well, thanks. It's a great sport."

"Good. Perhaps we'll see you here in the future then." Addressing the men, he said, "Will you fellows have your usual poison?"

"No, for tonight I think I'll have a brandy alexander," Cee Jay said.

"Very yummy. And for you sir?"

"I don't know what a brandy alexander is; but if he's having one, make it two."

"Why did I know you would say that?" The waiter said. "And for you, young man?"

"Tonight, I think I would like a hot cider, please"

"mmm. Since you said 'please,' I think I can get that for you. Say, which one of these two handsome men is your father?"

"I am," said Jamie.

"I thought so," Daniel said with a smile. "Karen, who is waiting on the other side of the room, was in the ratskeller last night. She said you had a beautiful voice and livened things up last night at karaoke. I guessed she was referring to you. I'm sorry I missed it."

"See, I told you that you were a hit," Cee Jay said.

"I can't understand why no one asked for my autograph," Jamie joked. "Usually, my fans are lined up after my shows."

The conversation over dinner that night was mostly about Jamie's vocal and dancing talents and how well Robbie did for just two days on the slopes. At one point in the conversation, however, Robbie had no idea what the men were talking about. Cee Jay had said that he thought Daniel was a friend of Dorothy and Jamie agreed, but neither said who Dorothy was and Robbie knew of no one by that name.

"Will, you be leaving early tomorrow or using your half-day ticket before checking out?" Daniel asked.

"We probably will hang around the game room and lobby or go swimming before we head home to Sussex County around noon," Cee Jay said.

"Just as good not to plan on skiing in the morning," their waiter said. "There is a weather alert for snow and sleet all night, turning to blizzard conditions during the day tomorrow. Drive home safely and come and see us again soon, okay."

On the way to their rooms, they stopped in the game room to play pool, but all four tables were in use, so the men decided to play shuffle board instead. Robbie watched the men play and challenged who ever would lose to play him. Cee Jay lost so it was he who got to play against Robbie, who also easily won.

"This kid is just too good for me," Cee Jay said in defeat.

In the elevator, Jamie asked Robbie if he wanted to come to his and Cee Jay's room to play cards for a while. Robbie agreed, but wanted to stop in his own room first. He said that he would be at 340 in a few minutes.

As soon as he knocked on the door of 340, Cee Jay opened it. Robbie was surprised to see Cee Jay had taken off all his clothes, including his shoes. All he was wearing were gym shorts. Robbie noticed how strong Cee Jay appeared. He had a fine-looking chest and arm muscles. *Yeah, he could pass for one of those GQ commercials also*, Robbie thought. He thought it would be inappropriate to mention anything even bordering on a compliment about his body. Entering the room more fully, he saw that Jamie, who was on the telephone, was similarly attired but he at least had a tee shirt that had 'Montclair State' written across the front.

"Here he is now," Jamie said to the person he had been talking to. "I'll put him on for you. "We're going to play cards for a while. I'll call you just before we leave the hotel tomorrow. Tell Barbie we send our love. Here's Robbie. Bye. See you soon. Love you."   He gave the phone to Robbie.

His mother asked if he were having a good time and how he liked skiing. "Your dad told me that you spent a lot of time with a boy from Mountain Ridge. Did he tell you that his mother goes to our church?"

Robbie was happy to hear his mother's voice, but he knew she wanted to talk about Cee Jay and dad.

"Robbie," his mother eventually got to the issue. "I guess you know now why your father wanted to go skiing with you and Cee Jay. We all thought it was the best way to tell you and Barbie. Honey, I know that right now it's hard for you to understand, but you and Barbie had to know the whole story. On Christmas, I told Cee Jay that if I had to share your father's love with anyone, I was glad it was with him. Cee Jay is a wonderful man, Robbie. Your sister is happy for both of them. We'll talk more when you guys get home. Make sure your dad drives safely. I'm glad they decided to take dad's pick up rather than Cee Jay's Chevy. I hear you may run into a big storm on the way home. Bye for now, son."

They played a few hands of black jack before they started to teach Robbie a game they played with his mother occasionally at home. The game, shanghai, seemed a bit confusing to Robbie after two hands, so he said that he was tired and it was getting late, so he left for 240.

He did wonder if they were going to finish all six hands of the game, go to sleep, or have sex

Ugh! he thought. And then he thought of Donavon Rice.

Chapter 7

THE RIDE HOME WAS treacherous. The Pennsylvania roads were slippery and, even with big, studded tires on his pickup. Jamie had a difficult time keeping on the road. Visibility was also poor, and the wipers couldn't keep up with the pounding sleet. Near Stroudsburg they pulled into a Burger King for a rest room break and hamburgers and coffee. Jamie also wanted to call Melissa to assure her they were okay and that they would probably be home around four o'clock and would be looking for a good, hot dinner. She asked if Cee Jay would be staying, but after briefly conferring with him, Jamie told his wife that Cee Jay was anxious to get Crackers, his golden retriever, out of the doggie hotel, and unwind in his own house.

On the other side of the Delaware Water Gap, the storm eased and turned to a light snow fall. Because of snow plows, the travel was slow; but they still were able to get to Cee Jay's house by three o'clock. Before they went inside, Jamie insisted on checking the garage to make sure Cee Jay's Chevy would start.

Robbie's first impression of Cee Jay's house was not what he had expected. He had the impression that the teacher would live in a one-story, modern place. Instead, it was a two-story center hall colonial, which was much older than his own house. The entire façade was stone which was set off by black shutters. The sides were masonry painted white with blue shutters. From the attached two-car, a covered walkway extended across the entire front. The house was set on a large, wooded lot amid pine and spruce trees. A gravel circular drive led from the county road.

Once the men were inside, Robbie felt very comfortable because in layout it was very similar to his own. The living room had a large fireplace and the ceiling was beamed. Except for the Persian rug in the center the floors were made of rough, polished plank. The furnishings gave the room a comfortable, lived-in feel. *Yeah, this is definitely a house for a mature, bachelor like Cee Jay,* Robbie thought. *I could see having a place like this myself someday.* He made a quick comparison to his own house and realized that the furnishings and decorations of the Roberts' household were probably chosen by his mother.

Cee Jay could sense that Robbie wanted to see more of his house. "Your dad and I will get some logs from the shed, and while he gets the fireplace going and makes some coffee for us, I'll take you on the twenty-five-cent tour of the Seton mansion," he said. "In the meantime, make yourself comfortable in one of the wing chairs." Robbie didn't need to be coached to select a large, brown leather recliner on the far side of the room. "mmm," Cee Jay said, "You are Jamie's son alright. That's his favorite chair, but you'll let him take it for today, right Jamie?"

Jamie snickered. "Let's get the firewood."

While the men were outside, Robbie sat comfortably in the chair and studied the room. He admired the large picture window at the other end which faced the front of the house as well as the picture window behind him which looked out on Cee Jay's spacious backyard.

"Yes," he said to himself, "Now I know why dad likes this chair."

A few minutes later both men carried in bundles of logs which they placed on a rack near the hearth. Jamie immediately started to prepare the logs to light the fireplace. "Are you ready for the twenty-five-cent tour, Robbie?" Cee Jay asked.

"Sure am," Robbie quickly responded getting off the recliner.

Opposite the living room, Cee Jay opened French doors into a library paneled with book shelves. The room contained a large desk, a file cabinet, and two chairs next to a table with a green shaded glass lamp. Behind the chairs was another picture window that matched the one in the living room. "I guess this is where you mark all your students' papers."

"Yep, this is where I read some interesting student work," Cee jay said, "and where I prepare those fascinating lessons which keep my students spellbound."

"Yah, right. I bet," Robbie said sarcastically but with a smile on his face.

Next to the library and open to the center hall was a formal dining room. The large table and a china closet were mahogany. Robbie admired the brass chandelier. He commented on how much he liked the wainscoting and the wallpaper above the railing which depicted a colonial village landscape. Off the dining room was a butler's pantry which led into a large, modern kitchen. Indicating a door on the right, Cee Jay explained that it was to the laundry room and garage. The long room was divided by a counter which separated the kitchen area from a morning or breakfast area. Sliding doors opened out to a covered patio and the back yard.

"This door is to the basement, but I won't show it to you now. Your dad keeps encouraging me to have it finished. Maybe one day I will; but right now it's just a high, and—thank god—dry empty space."

Another door between the breakfast room and kitchen led them back to the center hall. Cee Jay opened a door under the stairs to reveal a large closet. On the left was a "powder room" as Cee Jay called it. This half bath was in front of the butler's pantry. "Ready to see the upstairs now?" Cee Jay said as he led the way. Robbie caught a glimpse of his father and a small flame in the fireplace as he bounded up the stairs behind the teacher.

At the top of the stairs was an alcove sitting area with a chair and small table and lamp. Robbie was impressed by the size of Cee Jay's bedroom. "Wow! You have a fireplace in your bedroom," he exclaimed.

Cee Jay chuckled. "I'll tell you a secret, Robbie. That fireplace was what sold me on this house. I really love it. It's right above the one down stairs in the living room. I think it's kind of sexy. Don't you?"

Robbie was startled by this admission from his father's lover. "Yeah!" he said with a broad smile and glint in his eye.

"Originally the house had a nursery here," Cee Jay explained as he took Robbie into an adjoining room, "but as you see, I've made it into a mini gym and TV room. The room had a treadmill and an exercise machine for chest and arm muscles. The master bath had a large tub as well as a walk-in shower and dual vanity sinks. The commode was in an enclosed area by itself within the bathroom. There was a quaint but fully furnished guest bedroom which had its own full bathroom.

On the way back downstairs, Cee Jay turned to Robbie. "Well, what do you think, young man: was the tour worth your quarter?"

"I really like your house, Dr. S. It's so...so...you. I can understand now why dad likes hanging out here so much."

"Well, you're always welcome too, Robbie; but I hope that your dad likes it here for more reasons than just the house."

Cee Jay led him back to the kitchen where they found Jamie on the telephone.

"Okay, honey. We'll be home in about an hour." Jamie paused. "I love you, too. Bye."

By way of explanation, Jamie looked at Cee Jay. "I just called the wife to tell her that we got to your place safe and sound, and that Robbie and I would be home soon. The coffee is ready, and I put out some cookies. The mugs are on the counter. I thought we could fill our cups in here and take them into the living room."

"Good man," Cee Jay said in agreement.

In the living room, Jamie took the recliner that Robbie had earlier. Cee Jay sat in one of the wing chairs by the front window and Robbie settled on the large sofa opposite the fireplace, which was now giving off warmth and a delicious pine aroma. The logs were crackling.

Robbie was the first to speak. "Dad, I have a question. In the kitchen just now, you told Cee Jay that you called 'the wife.'"

"Yes, I probably did refer to your mother as my wife. She is. What's your question?"

"Well, for starters, what would you call Cee Jay, if you two were married?"

"Well, we are not married and even if we were, I wouldn't refer to him as 'my wife' or 'husband.' I might use words such as 'male lover' or just plain 'lover.' 'Partner' seems appropriate. I think Cee Jay would take offense if I called him my 'better half.' …I know I would." Jamie looked over to Cee Jay who was smiling. "Help me out here, buddy. How should we refer to one another? And what are you thinking with that silly ass grin on your face?"

"It's really just a matter of semantics, Robbie," Cee Jay began. "It really doesn't matter what we call one another as long as we truly love one another. Jamie, I was just thinking. Do you remember the two guys who lived above me in Greenwich Village, New York; their names were Paul and George?"

"Sure, the baseball players who played for La Bar. One of them, I think it was George, was hit by a line drive straight to his temple and died on the mound."

"Right. They were deeply in love. They were happier together than many married couples I've met before or since. Paul had a strange name for George though. Do you remember it, Jamie?"

This time it was Jamie who smiled. "Yeah. I haven't thought about it in years, but I do remember now. He always referred to his lover as 'Dip Shit.' How the hell did he ever get that name?"

"I don't know, but even at George's memorial service, Paul called him 'Dip Shit' in the most loving way imaginable." Cee Jay paused. "They first met while playing baseball at Rutgers, but didn't hook-up until a few years later when they ran into one another at La Bar. If they could have gotten married, those two would have been the first two in line." He paused again. "Maybe someday...maybe even in your life time, Robbie, it may be possible for gay people to legally marry." He chuckled. "But in your dad's case and mine, it would be polygamy, so under no circumstances would we ever get married."

"Son, Cee Jay was quite a gay activist in his day. He was actually at The Stonewall Riots."

"Stonewall? Riots? I have no idea what you're talking about," Robbie admitted.

"The Stonewall was a gay bar near where Cee Jay used to live in Greenwich Village in New York. In June of 1969 the police raided the bar, but the gay patrons had had it with police harassment and began demanding their rights. There were many gay bars, gay bath houses, and warehouse piers along the river in 1969 that the police could have—and should have—raided, but they chose The Stonewall. I guess the owners hadn't paid their 'protection money.' The gay people in the bar started fighting with the police. Then went outside into the street and actually began to riot. This marked the beginning of the whole gay rights movement. Which is, of course, still being played out."

"Wow! I never heard of it before. It's interesting. Was that the bar where you two met?"

Cee Jay answered. "No, we met years before Stonewall at another place called La Bar, which was two or three blocks away. Actually, I was not living in New York at the time of the riots. I just happened to be there by accident on the night of the rioting."

"Gosh! Mild-mannered Dr. Cee Jay Seton rioting. I can't picture it! Were you arrested and put in jail?"

Cee Jay laughed. "No. Nothing so glamorous. I was one of the hundreds of people who stood in the street and cheered and jeered, though. I never threw anything or broke or burned anything." He smiled. "Those were the days though, weren't they, Jamie?"

"Sure were."

"Remember all those characters at La Bar. All the talk, the guys making connections. It certainly was a popular place back in the Sixties. Many famous people frequented La Bar. I have fond memories of you, me,…the guys at the bar."

"And God," Jamie added.

"Indeed," Cee Jay said. "Oh, the tales that could be told from a Greenwich Village bar.

Sounds like the title of a good book. Doesn't it?"

"Yeah. You should write it, Cee Jay."

"Who knows? Maybe I will someday."

Both men were wrapped in their own thoughts for a minute.

It was Robbie who broke the silence. "Dad, it's getting late. We don't want mom to start worrying about us."

"Yes, and Cee Jay better get to the doggie hotel before they charge you another night for Crackers," Jamie said, "and I did tell Melissa we would be home around four, so we should be going." To Robbie's amazement his father grabbed Cee Jay and gave him a big bear hug which reminded him of the one Donavon had given him at the Manor. But the two men did more. They actually kissed on the lips! And in front of the startled Robbie. Robbie was speechless at first, but to break his own confusion, he said, "Ah, guys? Do you mind? I'm here you know?"

"No, I will not let you kiss my lover, Robbie. Eat your heart out." Jamie said jokingly.

"Good bye," Cee Jay said holding out his hand and shaking Robbie's. "Don't mind your father, Robbie. He's just an over grown teenager ostentatiously displaying his emotions," he said smiling at both Robbie and Cee Jay. "I really enjoyed our quality time together, Robbie. I hope that it helped you to understand our love for one another. Feel free to come here and visit any time you want or talk to me about anything."

Jamie and Robbie rode the short distance to their own house in silence. Robbie was still trying to process the whole thing between his father and Cee Jay. Jamie was a guy who was not afraid of showing his emotions and he was a good man with strong feelings of loving most people. Robbie liked Cee Jay, but the thought of his father being bisexual; that was something he knew he had to outwardly accept, like it or not. He wondered if he could ever fully accept it in his mind and heart, however.

Jamie was concentrating on the beauty of the area. The trees and fields were covered in the glow of freshly fallen snow. Jamie's heart was filled with love. He loved his family, he loved Cee Jay, and he loved this area. He thought of how different this beautiful area of New Jersey was from the dirty streets and decrepit tenements of Canarsie, Brooklyn, in which he had been a boy. Silently, he thanked God for all that he now enjoyed. He knew his wife appreciated him for who he was; he prayed that his children would now also.

As he drove into his driveway, Jamie broke the silence and said aloud, "God is good."

Robbie was startled by the break in the silence and shook his head. "What?"

Jamie extended both hands. "Just look around you, Robbie."

His son did, and he knew what Jamie meant, and he was happy.

Later that night, Robbie was in his room working on a new model airplane he left unfinished from Christmas. Barbie knocked on his door and entered with a smile on her face. Without being invited, she sat on his bed. Robbie looked up at her from his desk. "Well, "Barbie said, "were you surprised to hear about dad and Dr. S?"

"Yes, but I guess there's nothing I can do about it. I'm just glad that mom and dad are not getting a divorce."

His sister ran her hand through her blonde hair. "Yeah, I'm glad that divorce is not in the picture too. I like Cee Jay, but I'd hate him if he ever came between mom and dad."

"Cee Jay seems pretty okay with the relationship as it is."

"It's mom, I'm concerned with. How can she sleep with dad knowing that he might prefer to be with Cee Jay? I certainly couldn't live with such a guy," Barbie admitted.

"Didn't mom tell you that dad was bi?"

"Yeah, but still…"

"Did she tell you that dad loved Cee Jay even before I was born, but they never had sex? Hell, dad told me that mom knew he was bi before they were even married."

"She did. She told me that dad had a lot of experiences with men before they were married, but that she loved him so much, she was willing to put that matter out of mind, even if dad told her from time to time about Cee Jay."

"Dad said that he hasn't been with anyone but mom since I was born."

"Yeah, mom pretty much told me the same thing."

"How does mom feel about Dr. S?" Robbie asked.

"She told me that if she had to share her love for dad with anyone, she was glad it was with Cee Jay. She told me she really likes him and that, believe it or not, is actually happy that dad met Cee Jay again after all these years." Barbie began to cry. "Mom is such a great woman. I wish," she sobbed, "I could be as strong…and loving…as she is."

""I think dad is, too," Robbie said.

Barbie got off the bed and put her arms around her brother. She kissed him on the cheek. "I love you, little brother, even if our family is a little crazy."

"Yeah, our extended family now." Robbie emphasized the word 'extended.'

Barbie was at the door but then turned around and came back to sit on the bed. With a look of a canary that just swallowed a goldfish, she said, "Dad told us that you met a classmate of mine at the Manor."

"If you mean Donavon Rice, yes."

"Had I known that Don was going to be there, I would have begged dad to go along with you guys."

"Why?"

"Because he's the hottest guy at Mountain Ridge, that's why."

"Oh! You think so?" Robbie paused. "Did you know that he built that bus stop shelter and bench across from the school on Elliot Street?"

"That one and a few others around town," she said.

"I didn't know that."

"Dah, Robbie, everyone knows that Don did that as an Eagle Scout project. How could you not know? You must be the only person in Mountain Ridge who didn't know who put up the bus shelters. Really, other than basketball do you know anything that goes on around school, Robbie?"

"Well, now I know that your teacher is a faggot and you have the hots for Don Rice."

Barbie put both hands loosely around her brother's neck. "And don't you dare mention either of those things to anyone else in the world, or I'll strangle you. Do you understand?"

Robbie removed her hands from his neck. "Okay. Now will you let me get back to putting this fuselage together?"

She kissed him gently on the head before starting to leave the room.

"Oh, sis," he called back to her, "did dad tell you that Don and I went swimming as well as skiing? I saw your 'hot' guy in a bathing suit. He's GQ material for sure."

"Ugh! Now you've given me something else to think about tonight."

"Pleasant dreams," Robbie said sarcastically but with a smirk on his own face.

Robbie thought about how his sister would have reacted if he told her about the hard-on he had, and what he did about it while thinking about Don two nights ago.

Chapter 8

Mountain Ridge High School was scheduled to play Frankford High on Friday night. This was one of the most important games of the season because if they could defeat the "Coal Diggers," the "Mountaineers could still stand a chance of winning the County. Robbie was disappointed that Coach Ryan called off practice on Monday. Coach had said that not enough boys were back after the Christmas/New Year's break. Robbie thought that excuse was 'a crock of shit.' He knew that the real reason was that team morale was very low; and that if the coach called a practice on the first day back, some of the players would not show. Robbie was happy that he was moved to varsity this year, but he knew the team sucked. Other than himself and his best friend and teammate, a guard, Roger Pucket, Robbie felt the team lacked spirit. They were terrible on the court last year, and this season didn't seem to be much better. They seemed to be playing the game just for fun; they didn't seem to care if they won or lost. He felt that maybe the coach was at fault. Everyone in the school knew that Coach Ryan had announced in September that he was retiring from teaching at the end of the year and moving to Florida. His apathy toward the game had affected his players.

Robbie thought the team was almost a joke. The guys seemed more interested in fooling around in the locker room and showers than seriously playing to win. Unfortunately, the coach and Roger, his fellow junior starter, were the two who got most of the ribbing. "Fuck it, Pucket! It's only a game!" almost became a slogan as well as a derogatory remark against one of their own. Coach Ryan himself was the butt of much of the rowdy team humor. Rumors had long been circulating in the school that Ryan was a "fairy" because one of the players from Frankford claimed to have seen the coach outside of Mattie's, a notorious gay bar in town. The coach never tried to stop the rumors; instead, he either paid no attention or came back with a biting remark of his own.

Robbie remembered a particular event that disturbed him last year. Occasionally, when the guys got too loud in the showers or locker room, the coach would come in yelling at them to quiet down and stop acting like wild jackasses. It was then that behind his back, the guys would make wise-ass remarks about his being a faggot.

One day after practice the guys were rough-housing in the shower and Coach Ryan came in to quite them down. A senior guy said, "Ah, coach, you don't have to come in here every time you hear a piss ant junior squeal like he's being fucked. Unless you come in to see our dicks?" Robbie was shocked by the remark, but even more surprised by Ryan's answer: "Ciccone, in your case I'd need my magnifying glass to see your dick." The team thought this was hilarious and couldn't stop laughing. Even Ciccone liked it and said "good one, coach!" Ciccone was not disciplined, but Robbie was upset by it and that evening he told his mother about what happened.

At first Melissa seemed disturbed but paused for a moment and then told her son: "Concentrate on playing the game as best you can, Robbie. Don't pay any attention to those stupid jerks. Let Coach Ryan handle it as he wants, but you shouldn't get involved." At the time Robbie was surprised by his mother's uncharacteristic reaction. He thought she would have been disturbed, but that was last season…before he found out about his father.

Robbie wanted to win the game on Friday, not only for the school but for his own pride and the pride of his dad, who would be there as he was for all home games. He also wanted to play well for Donavon Rice. Donavon had told Robbie that he was watching him and thought that he was a good basketball player. Yes, Robbie wanted to live up to Don's expectations and impress his new, older friend. Before he met him at the Manor, Robbie didn't notice Donavon Rice, but now he wanted to see him in the gym on Friday.

The truth of the matter was that Robbie wanted to see Don every day. On Monday, he did not see him at all. But Robbie saw him in the hall Tuesday morning, and either Don didn't see him or deliberately avoided running into him. On Wednesday, Robbie wanted to go up to him in the cafeteria, but because Don was at a senior table joking with some of the other football jocks, he decided against it. At Thursday's skull-session Robbie was thinking more about Don than what Coach Ryan's assistant was saying about his scouting report of the Frankford "Diggers." By Friday Robbie was obsessing over whether Don would be at the game that night.

As usual at home games, Jamie drove Robbie to the school by 6:30 and then went on to meet Cee Jay in his office. The two men liked to get their favorite spot midway up the bleachers near center court before the team came out for the introductions and warm-up exercises. When Robbie was introduced over the PA, there was considerable applause and yelling. Looking up, Robbie noticed that most of the noise was coming from the middle of the stands.

His dad and the teacher were as boisterous as any of the teenagers in the gym every time he sunk a basket during the warm-up. Robbie was grateful that his dad was there; it made him feel proud and encouraged him to play his best. *All the three-pointers I make tonight are dedicated to you, dad,* he thought to himself. Finally, just as he was going to huddle for a team message from Coach Ryan, Robbie caught a glimpse of Donavon Rice at the door to the gym. Don was wearing his green and gold varsity football jacket as were the three or four other seniors in his posse. *All my two-pointers will be dedicated to you, Don,* Robbie thought just as the buzzer sounded.

The first quarter belonged to Mountain Ridge, 24-10. Robbie scored outside twice and had two layups and three points on the line. He had his all-time best quarter. Roger was fouled three times also and Hunter Brown, a senior, got two lay-up shots. During the second quarter the Diggers picked up their pace and the period ended tied at 40-40. At the buzzer, Robbie took a quick look around the bleachers to espy Don, but he could not see him or any of the footballers.

Coming back out after the half, Robbie saw his dad and Cee Jay, but sitting next to Jamie was Donavon Rice. All three high-fived one another when they saw Robbie. Don and Jamie gave loud whistles which embarrassed the hell out of Robbie. He didn't know what to make of it. *Oh, God: top senior jock with my dad and his teacher lover. What the hell's going to happen?*

What did happen was that Robbie played his very best game, scoring a team high of 33 points for the night. His efforts aroused the team spirit and the Mountaineers finished 54-48.

The gym went wild at the final buzzer. Robbie caught a glimpse of Don and his father hugging as he was swept into celebration with his teammates.

After a quick shower and dressing back to his regular clothes, Robbie went to meet his father in the gym lobby. Robbie was startled to see that Donavon and Cee Jay were with him. Jamie gave his son a bear hug. Cee Jay shook his hand and congratulated him for playing so well. Donavon shook his hand but also padded his back with the other hand. "Roberts, you played really well tonight," Don said.

Jamie informed Robbie that while they were waiting for him to change, he volunteered to drive Donavon home because his friends left at half-time and he had no transportation.. Cee Jay said that he had to get home to take care of Crackers.

Leaving the gym that night, accompanied by his father and Donavon Rice, Robbie could not have been prouder. He also felt that Donavon would be a good friend for a long time.

Chapter 9

ROBBIE THOUGHT THAT AFTER Friday's win, Don would call him, and they would make plans to hang out sometime. After all, Jamie had given him his card and told him to give "us" a call as Don got out of the pick-up. Robbie thought that the least Don could do was to greet him in the halls at school or come up to say "Hi!" in the cafeteria. Robbie saw Donavon a few times. Once he was actually talking to Barbie at her locker, but he never acknowledged Robbie's presence.

As the week wore on, Robbie was disappointed and saddened by Donavon's lack of interest.

This Friday night's game was away at Mohawk, so rather than going with his dad and Cee Jay, he had to take the team bus. On away games, his mother usually picked him up at the school for the ride home. Occasionally she would also drive Roger home. He did not expect many fans except the cheerleaders from Mountain Ridge to be at the game against "The Lakers." Certainly, he did not expect to see Donavon Rice there.

At practices during the week, Robbie thought that the team was more serious and focused on winning. Perhaps the win and the fact that the high scorer was only a junior center invigorated the team and encouraged them to play better.

Robbie took this game very seriously and gave it his best. The entire team played well. Even Coach Ryan at halftime told his players that "The Lakers" were playing a sloppy game. He pointed to the two traveling violations they made and the many fouls they committed. Obvious to all, was the flagrant foul charged to a "Laker" who actually punched Roger Pucket. The game became a nail-biter during the second half; but in the final seconds, Mountain Ridge pulled ahead and won by four points. Robbie again was the team leader by chalking up a total of 28 points. He had won the respect of his teammates who had been critical of his being moved from JV center to varsity so soon. Even Roger, who had been punched during the game, managed 16 points. On the bus back to Mountain Ridge, there were no "Fuck it, Pucket! It's only a game!" jeers. All the guys were jubilant on the way home; but by the time they reached the school parking lot, they were all quiet and very tired. Perhaps, some of them were thinking, as Robbie was, of next week's game against Sparta Catholic and the possibility of playing in the County final four.

Robbie was glad that his mother was already at the lot when the bus pulled up. She had the heater on in the car. She told him that she and his dad had listened to the game on the radio station out of Newton. Mellissa hugged him and said that she was very proud of him. She said that Jamie was already talking about the County Championship game.

The Roberts family usually spent Saturdays in the same way. Jamie would go to his office to make telephone calls to new prospective customers. Melissa and Robbie would go with him; she would clean the office and catch up on any financial matter left undone during the week, and Robbie would do chores assigned by either of his parents. Barbie stayed at home to do house cleaning chores.

When the phone rang in the morning, Jamie, thinking the call would be from a customer, automatically picked up the phone. It wasn't a customer.

"Good morning, Mr. Roberts. Donavon Rice here."

"Oh, hello, Don. How are you?"

"I'm very well, thank you, sir. And you?"

"Fine, fine. What can I do for you, Don?"

"Well, actually I'm calling to congratulate Robbie about last night's game."

"Great game! Robbie's right here. I'll put him on for you."

When Robbie heard Don's name, and then his own, he became flustered. He was both excited and nervous as he took the phone from his father.

"Hello," he said weakly. "What's up, Don?"

"I just called to tell you that I heard the game on the radio last night. You played one hell of a game, Roberts. I wish I could have been there to see it…er…you!"

"Thanks. The team is improving."

"Say, Roberts, your dad told me last week that you enjoy building model air planes; just happens I got one as a Christmas present from my cousin. I was wondering if I could come over to your house this afternoon and you could help me put it together."

"It's okay with me, but I'll have to check with my parents. I usually go to dad's business to help out on Saturdays." He turned to Jamie. "Dad, is it okay if Don comes here this afternoon? He has a model plane he wants help in building."

It was Mrs. Roberts who answered for her husband. "There's not much to do today in the office. I could drive you back home by one o'clock."

Jamie nodded in agreement. "I'll take the Ram and come home later. So, yeah, tell Don to come over around two."

Robbie couldn't understand why his father had told Don that he liked modeling. He wondered what else he told him. He hoped it was nothing about Cee Jay. He did think it would be fun to hang out with Don for a while. The thought came to him that it might be fun to bond with Don as well as some parts of an air plane. That morning at Roberts Construction and Contracting, he couldn't wait until he got back home and could meet with Don.

Robbie was looking out his bedroom window, when a few minutes before two o'clock, he saw Donavon bicycle up to the front of the house and lock the bike to a wrought iron fence behind the bushes in front of the porch.

It was Barbie who answered the door. Robbie heard the classmates chatter a little and then his sister yelled up the stairs to tell him that Don was here. Robbie ran back to his desk and pretended that he was engrossed in reading a book when Don knocked on his bedroom door.

"Come on in," he said as casually as he could, but he didn't have to because Don was already half way in the room. Turning to see him, Robbie's heart skipped a beat. Don opened his green and gold jacket to reveal a plaid shirt and tight, blue jeans. Robbie wished that he had jeans that showed off his crotch so well. Don quickly put the box containing his model plane on the bed and then tossed his bike helmet next to it. He rifled his hands through his thick hair in an effort to straighten it out. Robbie caught the scent of Axe.

Both boys were tense as they sat at the edge of the bed looking at the box of a model of a World War Two B-29. Eventually, Robbie got another chair so they could both sit at the desk. From his closet, he got his kit containing several Exacto knives, different glues, and other materials for modeling.

Robbie was pleased to see how interested Don was in his hobby. He seemed to be a quick learner. After a while when a stretch seemed necessary, Robbie asked if he could get him a coke. The older boy quickly accepted the offer.

Returning to his room with the drinks, Robbie found Don admiring the models and small trophies he had on his bookcase.

"Which one is your favorite?" Don asked holding one of the air craft in his hands.

"I like all of them, but my favorite is a remote-controlled DC-3 that my dad has hanging down at his warehouse. I made it a few years ago and every spring my dad and I take it to the park to fly. That's how I became interested in actually flying and wanting to become a pilot. As a Christmas present, Cee Jay…er…I mean, Dr. S, gave me a flight-simulation CD that's really cool." Suddenly Robbie realized that he should not have mentioned his dad's lover.

"Cool! Does Dr. Seton go to the park with you and your dad to fly your remote model?"

"No," Robbie paused. "But maybe this year he will."

"Awesome! Maybe I could join you," Don said enthusiastically.

"Yeah," Robbie responded before quickly changing the subject back to constructing Don's B-29 model.

The hours he spent with Don that Saturday afternoon seemed to go too quickly, and at five o'clock Don announced that he should start pedaling home. It was agreed that they would finish adding a few accessories and paint the model some other time. Robbie suggested that Don keep it on his bookcase until it was finished. Down stairs Melissa came out of the kitchen to introduce herself to Donavon. "My husband has told me so much about you, Donavon. He told me that you met skiing last month," she said shaking his hand. "Please come again to visit with Robbie and us."

Robbie seemed to think that Barbie suddenly came from out of nowhere to also say goodbye. "Hey," she said to Don. "Nice to see you out of Dr. S's class."

Don's parting words to them were: "Tell Mr. Roberts that I said hello and was sorry to have missed seeing him today."

Closing the door, Mrs. Roberts said, "What a nice boy. I hope you two become good friends, Robbie."

"So do I," Barbie said with a smile on her face, but meaning more than her mother.

Chapter 10

DURING THE FOLLOWING WEEK, Robbie was too busy concentrating on Friday night's game against Sparta Catholic to give much thought to Donavon. Coach Ryan pushed his boys hard at practice every day. They responded by meeting his challenges. It seemed that now everyone wanted to win that final game of the regular schedule. One of the senior forwards did say, "Fuck it, Pucket; it's only a game," but even he got psyched for the county-four playoffs. Each day by the time practice was over and he got home, had dinner, and did his homework, Robbie was too tired to do anything but collapse in bed. He never tried to work on a model, but once or twice did look at Don's B-29.

Robbie began looking at other things during the week. Mainly, he was looking at his own cock and face. Each morning as he showered, he ran his hand across his penis and got an instant pleasurable response. Although he noticed that he was getting erect, he felt happy just being aware that it was happening; but he didn't have the time or real desire to jerk off. He was just anxious to get to school and practice. Robbie had always been conscious of the few pimples on his face, but now decided to really do something about them. Rather than squeezing whiteheads, he really scrubbed his face thoroughly with soap. He actually asked his sister for something she had used. She gave it to him, but said that she didn't think his condition was that bad; however, she did tell him to comb his hair. He took her advice and started brushing his hair in the morning.

The whole school seemed to be getting into the spirit of a basketball victory. A few girls had actually spoken to him in the halls, and a few guys gave him high-fives and wished him luck.

On Wednesday, almost the impossible happened; Johnny Shaw, the senior forward who usually started the "Fuck it, Pucket" chants actually sat at Robbie and Roger's table for lunch. Robbie didn't care that Donavon Rice remained with his football pals and never called or recognized him around school. Once Robbie thought, *Fuck you, Rice! You're no prize. I can make other friends.*

The game was at Sparta Catholic, so once again, Robbie had to take the team bus to the game. Jamie told him that both him and Cee Jay would be at the game, however. When the bus got back to Mountain Ridge, he would be waiting to take Robbie home. Jamie made a point of saying that Cee Jay would be going to the game in his own car.

Sparta Catholic High School was a new, big school that drew students from all over Sussex and Passaic Counties. In its two years of existence it had developed a reputation for an excellent academic program. It was one of the few catholic preparatory schools in the state to be co-educational. The school was also known for its sports program, particularly track and swimming. It was the only school that had both a separate theater wing and an indoor swimming pool. Jamie and Mellissa had thought of sending Robbie there, but the tuition was more than they could afford at the time and the school did not have school buses. Commuting would have presented huge problems. Both parents were happy with the education Barbie was getting at Mountain Ridge, so they determined that Robbie would also. When the Mountaineers arrived, the boys were in awe of how modern and nice the school was. Instead of vinyl tile, the hallways had terrazzo and the classrooms and locker rooms actually had carpeting. They noted that the shower room had individual partitions. "Don't let all this elegance frighten you, boys," Coach Ryan had said. "Their basketball record of eight /four and seven/ five this year pretty much matches ours, but they lost the last two while we won our last two. Now let's make it three in a row and go onto the county finals." All the players knew that if they won this game, it would be the first time in five years that Mountain Ridge would reach the post season. Robbie was determined that they would.

When the team entered the gym, they were surprised how crowded it was on both sides. Sparta Catholic fans were forced to sit on the visitors' side because their own side was packed. During the introduction and warm up, Robbie spotted his dad and Cee Jay in the same position they occupied at home. Although he recognized many of the Mountain Ridge faculty and students, he did not see Donavon Rice. To himself, he thought: *You're no prize, Rice! I'm playing this one for myself, my dad, and—yes—for Cee Jay too.*

"What the hell! Is Jesus on their side?" Shaw remarked seeing the Catholic school boys get down on their knees in huddle before the game began.

"Shaw, you're going to be on your ass, if we don't win this one," Robbie found himself saying and then thinking he was pretty macho for saying it.

It was evident almost from the start that Mountain Ridge would win. They had greater height. They out-ran, and out-scored the boys in blue and white. Robbie's aim was perfect, and he made two baskets from the outside within the first ten minutes.

At the beginning of the second quarter, Roger Pucket fouled the opposition's center who went to the line to shoot two. The center made the sign of the cross before attempting both shots, which hit the rim and bounced back. Shaw grabbed the ball after the second ball missed and jeered, "Huh, now we know what side Jesus really is on!"

Robbie's quick retort was something he heard Cee Jay say a few times, but modified. "That's an ostentatious display of wishful thinking."

The forward dribbled the ball a few times in place, and took off like lightning down to the opposite side of the court and dunked the ball through the hoop. The Spartan team stood in awe of Shaw's speed.

At half time the score was Mountaineers 42, Blue and White 28. Jamie, Cee Jay and all the other Mountain Ridge fans were whooping it up, while the Spartan Catholics seemed to be in shock. A cheerleader, who was in one of Robbie's classes, ran up to him as he was leaving the court. She gave him a big bear hug, and practically screamed "I love you, Roberts!" Robbie could feel her breasts on his chest and saw the braces on her teeth.

During half-time Coach Ryan soberly went over some of the plays which he had drilled them on during the week. Based on what he saw during the first half, the scouting reports were right-on and the new plays should work. He may have felt that they were now in line for the post season, but he didn't want his boys to become overly-confident, so he played it cool and didn't show his own emotions. "Now, let's get out there and execute them!" the coach roared.

The Blue and White team managed to show improvement during the third quarter but still were trailing the Mountaineers at the end. Roger Pucket made several excellent free throws from the line and broke his own record. Robbie padded his friend on the ass and made sure that the catholic team knew this junior broke a record.

When the game ended, the Mountain Ridge fans, coach, players, and cheerleaders all were jumping and screaming. They knew that for the first time in five years they were going to play at the Sussex County Community College next week for the County Championship. All the players were hugging one another. Robbie made sure that he had a chance to hug his coach before Ryan was pulled aside by a newspaper reporter for an interview. Robbie was then virtually attacked by two cheerleaders. One of the girls was so happy she was crying. The other cheerleader said, "Win the next one and I'm all yours, Robbie."

"Don't believe her, Roberts," Shaw said rescuing him from the cheerleaders. "She says that to all the players." He turned her around and kissed her. "Don't you, baby?" Turning to put an arm around Robbie, he added," but she never does put out except for me. Isn't that right, baby?"

Robbie dropped the conversation in his enthusiasm to hug Roger.

The celebration continued in the visitors' locker and shower rooms, but the team bus became eerily quiet as it pulled away from Sparta Catholic High School. Everyone knew that winning the next game would not be as easy.

Robbie slept later than usual on Saturday. When he went down to the kitchen, he found the family already having their breakfast. His mother said that they didn't want to disturb him. "We know that you were probably exhausted after last night's game. Besides, your father and I decided that there isn't much to do at the office, so there's no need to go there today. Dad's going to Cee Jay's. I'll take care of the house work here today, and you and Barbie can catch up on some homework."

"That's okay with me," Robbie shrugged.

"By the way, Donavon Rice, called you about an hour ago. I didn't want to waken you, so he left his telephone number. I put it on the hall table for you."

"Okay. I'll call him later." Robbie didn't want to make it sound as though he was excited to get this news. But he was. "He probably wants to come over to work on his model B-29."

"Or to tell you what a great game you played last night," Jamie said.

"Whatever," Robbie said as nonchalantly as possible.

"Invite him over," Barbie said. "There's something I've been wanting to ask him that I can't ask at school."

"What's so important that you can't ask him at school?" their mother asked.

"Well, dad's buddy," She emphasized the word 'buddy' before continuing. "Dr. Cee Jay Seton gave our class a really big project to complete for graduation. We have to do it with a partner from the class. I'd like to work with Donavon, but I haven't had a chance to ask him if we could be partners. Cee Jay wants us to pick our own partners and choose our projects together."

"That sounds good, honey. Do you have any ideas on your topic yet?" Jamie asked.

"Yes, dad, I do, but I want to run it through Donavon to get his reaction first. He may already have a partner that he's working with."

"So why do you want to work with Don?" Robbie interrupted.

"Because he's the smartest kid in the class. Besides me, of course."

"Of course," Robbie interjected.

"Well, he is the smartest boy in the class. His opinions are always well thought out, he can present things very well, and I know he does power point and slide presentations well. Cee Jay said our projects had to include visuals as well as a paper. Also, a few months ago, Don and Cee Jay had a discussion in class about something that caused me to do some research on it myself. So, I think Cee Jay would approve my topic idea, and Donavon might like it too." She paused and then lowered her voice. "And I think I would like working with him."

"mmm. Always the conniving female," Robbie said.

"Well, it all sounds very good to me," his mother said, reassuring Barbie. "Robbie, you be sure to call Donavon and invite him over here today."

"But don't you dare tell him about your conniving sister's plan. Let her do that herself when Don gets here," Jamie said.

"Thanks, dad," Barbie said.

Robbie deliberately waited until noon to call Don. He didn't want to seem too anxious, even though he was. Don's phone only rang once before he picked up.

"Roberts! Great to hear from you. Congrats on last night's game. I knew you would lead those guys to play better. This is the first time in—what—five years that Mountain Ridge made it to the finals. You must really be psyched. "

"Yeah, everyone on the team played well last night."

"Sorry I couldn't be there in person, buddy; but I was listening to it on the radio."

"Oh, you weren't there? A lot of Mountaineers were."

"No, I had to work last night."

"I didn't know you had a job."

"Yeah, I've been working evenings at 'the golden arches' in town since football season ended. I thought you knew that. I normally have Friday nights off, but staff has been calling in with all kinds of excuses and my boss calls me to fill in a lot lately. I could use the extra time because I'm saving for a car and college next year."

Suddenly, Robbie realized that there was a lot more that he didn't know about Donavon.

"I guess you want to come over this afternoon to work on your model plane again."

"No, I can't today. I already promised Jennifer O'Brian I'd go with her to the mall this afternoon. How about tomorrow though? Is one o'clock good for you?"

"Ah, okay. See you at one tomorrow then." Robbie spoke hesitatingly as he contemplated the name 'Jennifer O'Brian.' Somehow that name seemed familiar.

"Great! See you tomorrow, buddy. Bye for now."

Later he asked his sister if she knew a girl by the name of Jennifer O'Brian.

"Dah! Honestly, Robbie some time I wonder what planet you're on. Everyone at Mountain Ridge knows that bimbo. She's a cheerleader and Student Council president. She's been out with every jock in school. For a while she was dating your teammate Johnny Shaw, but word has it that she now has her claws out for your pal, Donavon Rice. Why do you ask?" She paused. "Oh, my God! Has she been trying to hit on you too?"

Robbie realized that the cheerleader who said that he 'could have her' and who Shaw had kissed after the game last night was Jennifer O'Brian. Robbie then remembered hearing her name a few times in the gym showers. "No, not me. But Donavon just told me that he couldn't come over here today because he has a date with her this afternoon."

"So, it is true! That bitch! Well, we'll see how long that little romance lasts."

"Why do you say that?"

"Donavon Rice is notorious for dating about as many girls as that bimbo O'Brian does guys. But Don never calls them after the first date. I don't know of anyone who ever went out with him twice, and I've heard he never gets to first base with any of his girlfriends."

Robbie again thought that there was a lot he didn't know about Donavon. He also realized that he never remembered having this kind of conversation with Barbie before. ...He liked it though. ...And he wanted to learn more about Donavon.

"So, is Don coming over to work on his model airplane some other time?" his sister asked while putting imaginary quotation marks with her fingers around 'his model airplane.'

"Yes, tomorrow afternoon around one o'clock."

"Good," was all his sister said and walked away.

Chapter 11

DONAVON RICE RODE HIS bicycle with joy on Sunday afternoon. Normally, it would still be cold and either raining, looking like it was going to rain, or snowing; but today felt like an April day rather than the first of March, which it was. The snow and its accompanying mud puddles were gone. It was warm enough for him to open his green and gold varsity jacket fully; the sides were flapping in the gentle breeze. As he rode through its streets, Donavon thought how lucky he was to be living in this town. He loved the small town's wide, tree-lined streets, the diversity of the architectural styles of its houses, the people who lived here, his school and his friends.

He knew that by now many of his friends had learned that he was with Jennifer O'Brian, the best-looking girl in the school, yesterday. It didn't matter that all they did was walk through the mall in the afternoon or that all he 'got' was a kiss; he knew his buddies would expand the story to include some exciting sexual fantasy of the 'date.' He knew that all the guys lied about their sexual exploits with girls, but Donavon knew many of them were still virgins, like himself. He was proud that at eighteen, almost nineteen, he was still a virgin; of course, he would never admit it to any of his teammates. Don felt that he was 'saving it' for the girl that he would marry. His catholic elementary education taught him that sex outside of marriage was a sin, but his own idea on that matter was that he probably would have sex with the girl he was planning on 'doing it' with for a lifetime. He had heard that a lot of couples found out too late that they were not sexually compatible. That, he thought, would never happen. He rationalized that he was too young to even get really involved with a girl. He had dated many females but never really felt the need or desire to go any further. He still had plenty of time to find the right girl for himself. As long as he dated and, therefore, put up a good front of being a 'real stud,' he didn't care. He still had the rest of senior year and at least four more years of college, so he was in no hurry, he thought, to get serious with anyone 'that way.'

Donavon was content in knowing that his applications to Rutgers and Montclair Universities were sent in. He was not going to an expensive school out of New Jersey, not only because he didn't want to go far from home, but also because he knew he could not afford to go out of state. Rutgers was his first choice. If he got a good football scholarship and one from the Boy Scouts they would help pay for tuition. He knew he stood a good chance of also getting an academic scholarship. Montclair State was a good back-up because he could live at home. But he really wanted to get away from his boring family. He knew that he could get some financial help to either university. "Hell," he thought "on the bases of Dr. Seton's recommendation alone I could get into Princeton. And judging from what Coach Goodman said about my athletic ability, I should get the Heisman Trophy. Earning an Eagle Badge should also help."

He was on his way to visit the Roberts family. He wondered if Robbie knew that he was not truthful about getting the model airplane as a Christmas present. When Mr. Roberts told him that Robbie's hobby was building models, He went to the hobby shop at the mall and bought it. That was only his excuse to get to know Robbie and the Roberts family better.

Barbie was pretty, intelligent, and known for speaking her opinions. She also had the reputation of being a virgin because she seldom, if ever, went to parties or dances. It didn't help socially that in the classroom she would always contradict the guys by saying something about so-and-so's opinion being chauvinistic. Donavon admired her perky attitude and ability to defend her own opinions. He wished his own mother had that quality. He had thought about going out with Barbie, but he was too awkward about asking her for a date. Meeting Robbie at the Pocono Manor Lodge with his father and his best friend, who was a teacher, presented a good opportunity.

For the last two years Don had been watching Robbie on and off the basketball court. He knew that Robbie was good and deserved to be moved into the Varsity center position even though he was only a junior. Robbie's cheerfulness and his ability to not just get along with others but also to lead them, reminded Donavon of himself. Robbie was his same height but a few pounds thinner. Donavon had often wished he had a younger brother, someone who would look to him for guidance and someone to play sports and hang out with. He wished he had someone to talk to and really level with. Don wished that Robbie were his brother. Don also liked Jamie. Mr. Roberts was a successful businessman and well known in the community. Don didn't know how old Jamie was, but he did think that he was good looking and physically fit for whatever his age was. He had noted that Jamie and his teacher, Dr. Seton, were often together at football and basketball games as well as other school functions. He was really surprised to see Dr. Seton with Robbie's dad at the Manor. Now, as he bicycled, he had a picture in his mind of how handsome both men were in bathing suits. He suspected that his teacher was a few years older than

Mr. Roberts, but he was still very attractive. At the Manor pool that night, Don had thought how all the girls at school would have swooned to catch a glimpse of Dr. S in a speedo. Don was curious to learn more about how these two men met and remained friends for so long. They seemed so similar, yet were obviously different. Jamie was into construction, while Dr. 'S' had a Ph.D. in literature. It dawned on Don that perhaps his relationship with Robbie could be like that between Dr. 'S' and Mr. Roberts.

Donavon thought of the Roberts family as Ozzie and Harriett. Mrs. Roberts was the perfect mom and Jamie Roberts the perfect dad. Robbie and Barbie were the all-American children of the family. They were very different from the Rice family. Donavon's step dad showed little interest in sports and even less in his step son. They seldom, if ever, had a man-to-man conversation. Never was the word 'sex' mentioned in the Rice household. Donavon thought of his own mother as being way too religious and old-fashioned. Other than church matters and her own household chores, Don's mother didn't seem to have many interests

Donavon rang his bicycle bell and waved to a friend that he saw getting out of a car with his family. The boy was dressed in a tie and jacket; Don thought that he was probably coming home from lunch after a church service. Don pedaled a little faster the last few blocks to the Roberts' house because he was anxious to get there, and he wanted to be right on time. He always thought that punctuality was a key to success.

Barbie opened the door for Donavon. She told him that Robbie was up in his room, but had agreed to let her meet with Donavon about their school project before he would work on his model. "I'd like to talk to you about something, Donavon. So let's go into the library." She led the way.

"What's up, Barbie."

"Please have a seat." She sat on a wing back chair next to the over-stuffed leather recliner she indicated for Don.

"You know that English project that Dr. Seton assigned?"

"How can I forget? He wants us to select a partner and a topic by next week. I have no idea on what to do for it."

"That's what I want to talk to you about, Don." She paused. "Do you have a partner yet?"

"No. I didn't make any definite commitment yet with anybody, but I did discuss it with two or three kids; but they don't have topics yet either."

"That's good, Donavon, because I would like you to be my partner, and I do have two possible topics that I think we might both like."

"Great!' Donavon said. "What are your ideas?"

"Well, the first one concerns John Milton. Using the outline that Seton gave us, we could give a brief over-view of his life and give a summary of *Paradise Lost*. Then, using the outline Cee Jay—err, I mean Dr. Seton—gave us we could analyze "Il Penseroso" and "L'Allegro" with music, pictures, and slides as a power point program."

"That sounds like a real winner, Barbie." He was pensive for a moment before adding, "What's the second topic you had in mind?"

"Well, actually it was you who gave me the idea for the second one. Remember about a month or so ago when we were studying *1984* in class you told Dr. Seton that many of George Orwell's predictions for the future seemed to be actually true today?"

Yes, and he told me to read another dystopian novel, *Brave New World*. But I never got around to reading it."

"Okay. But Dr. S also suggested that you also read Huxley's sequel to it, *Brave New World Revisited*, in which he talks about the precise ideas you had for *1984* and civilization today." Barbie paused long enough to give Don a moment to think about what she had said. "Well, I decided to read both the book and the sequel, *Revisited*. I think our project could be an analysis of both Orwell and Huxley's works, which illustrate that to a large extent we are already living in the dystopian civilization both originally predicted as science fiction."

Donavon seemed to be in deep thought before responding. "I like your second idea better," he said.

"Okay. Why?"

"For starters, if we did anything with Milton's *Paradise Lost*, we might get ourselves in way over our heads, and the class might find it boring. I probably would myself. The imagery in "L'Allegro" and "Il Penseroso" is great and we could easily find illustrations for both poems. But we studied both poems in class and our analysis would have to be based on Seton's outline, so he might think we didn't do enough original research and put enough of our own creativity into it. I think it would be fun to do, but Dr. S and the class might think it was too easy.

"Your second idea on dystopian literature has a lot of merit. The class would be interested because it is pertinent to the world we live in today. Dr. Seton would be pleased to see that we did take his challenge to read both Aldous Huxley works as well as returning to and expanding what we did in class. I've seen *Brave New World* on a few reading lists recommended for college, so I and the class might find it helpful. This project would certainly require some research and creativity. Illustrating the books in a slide or power point program would also be interesting and fun."

Barbie Roberts smiled. "Well, Donavon. You have convinced me. So, it's a go then? You and I are partners on dystopia?" She extended a hand shake.

"Partners," he said shaking her hand and thinking to himself that he would really like working with her.

"Could we meet in the library tomorrow after school to write up the proposal for Dr. S?" she asked.

"You betcha!" Donavon assured here. "Now I better get upstairs to see Robbie and get that B-29 model finished." Donavon bounded up the stairs to Robbie's room.

Barbie was very pleased with herself. Now that she was partnered with Donavon Rice she knew they would get an "A" on the project. She also knew that she would get to know the real Donavon Rice better. She smiled and softly to herself said, *Eat your heart out, Jennifer O'Brian.*

Upstairs, Don found that Robbie was already working on the model. He had assembled the wheels and was now in the process of gluing them to the fuselage. He got up to give Donavon the desk chair. "We could finish the plane this afternoon. Once the landing gear is firm, we can paint it and you can put on the decals. I have some brushes you can use to paint it."

Robbie showed the senior how to apply the paint and then sat on the edge of his bed. Don told him about the plans he made with Barbie to work on the English project. Donavon also talked about Robbie's improvement on the basketball court and how he felt about the up-coming game. Eventually, the conversation included Johnny Shaw and Jennifer O'Brian. "How was your date with her yesterday?"

"It was okay, I guess. We just walked around the mall for a while. Nothing special."

"Do you believe what Johnny told me about her putting the make on me and all the school's athletes."

"Yeah, I kind'a do. I know she tried to get with me during the season a few times, but I put her off until last week. As for Shaw, he has a big mouth."

"Do you like her?"

"I don't know what you mean by 'like', Roberts. I guess she's okay. But if you mean: will I ask her to go out with me again, the answer is 'no.' "

That answer pleased Robbie, but he didn't quite know why. While putting on a wing decal insignia, Donavon accidently cut his finger. Seeing a few droplets of blood, Donavon put the Exacto knife down and sucked the blood off his finger. Almost instantly, Robbie picked up the knife and deliberately gave himself a small cut on his own finger. To Don's amazement, Robbie grabbed his finger and then rubbed his own blood over Don's.

"What?…What did you do that for?" Donavon asked.

"So we could be blood-brothers."

Robbie said it so innocently and genuinely that Don was tempted to instantly kiss him; but realizing that he couldn't do that, after a moment he said softly: "Yeah I'd like that. Now we are blood brothers."

Someone knocked on the door. It was Melissa, Robbie's mother. "Hello, Donavon. I just came up to tell you guys that dinner will be ready in a few minutes. I hope you will stay to eat with us, Donavon. My husband just called me to say that he and Dr. Seton were going to a restaurant for dinner, so we have plenty of food here."

"Please stay, Don," Robbie pleaded. "My mom makes a great lasagna. I know that Barbie would like you to stay also."

"Hey, thanks very much, Mrs. Roberts; but I told my mother that I'd be home for dinner around five o'clock. She'll be mad if I'm not home for her special, chicken cacciatore, which she knows I love."

"Well, we can't disappoint your mother, Don. I understand. We'll just have to plan to have you here for dinner some other time. I'm sure my husband would prefer to be here to enjoy your company also."

"Thanks again for the invite, Mrs. Roberts. I'll arrange that with Robbie…or Barbie."

"Well, goodbye for now. Dinner in fifteen minutes Robbie," she said leaving the boys.

The model B-59 was finished. "How are you going to get it home?" Robbie asked. "It's too big to take on your bicycle."

"mmm." Donavon was thinking.

"Perhaps my dad could take it over to your house in his pick-up. I'm sure he wouldn't mind."

"No, I have a better idea, Robbie. Keep it here on top of your bookcase. I want you to keep it."

"But, why? It's your first model. Don't you want to keep it?"

"I want you to have it for helping me build it, Robbie. Also, every time you look at it, you'll think of me...your blood-brother."

Chapter 12

On Monday during homeroom period it was announced that Mountain Ridge would play Sparta Regional High on Saturday in the first game of the two-day County championship. The winner of that game would play against the team that won the second game between Ogdensburg and High Point Regional. The final game was scheduled for Sunday afternoon.

Coach Ryan and the entire team were hoping that they would play Ogdensburg rather than Sparta in their semi-final. While Ogdensburg and High Point Regional had similar win/ loss records for the regular season, Ogdensburg had the reputation for being a weaker team. Sparta Regional had won the County trophy last year and had an outstanding record again this year. All five starters were seniors.

The Mountaineers were happy just to make it to the finals for the first time in five years.

The coach was determined to close out his career with a good record. Robbie and the entire team had improved their attitudes and records. By Monday afternoon, the cheerleaders were busy making posters, and by Tuesday the school was filled with signs assuring everyone that the green and gold would defeat Sparta Regional. Principal Warren announced that on Friday afternoon there would be a pep rally in the gym. Although there always was a pep rally for the opening of all the sports, no one could remember a second pep rally for any one sport other than football.

Coach Ryan called practices every day from 3:00 to 5:30. The team did running exercises, dribbling exercises, passing, and shooting from every possible ankle. The coach had the second stringers and the starters play mixed in quarters. Each day they spent time reviewing rules and the scouting reports. They watched a video tape of the Sparta Regional team that was made at the final game last year. Most of that team would still be playing this year, so the coach pointed out the strengths and weaknesses he observed in each player and told his own players what to expect on Saturday.

By the time Robbie got home each day, he was almost too tired to have dinner with his family. He did only the minimum amount of homework before hitting the sheets. He noted that he got up in darkness and got home in darkness. He had no life outside of school. His entire mind and body were focused on Saturday's game. While he admired the extra attention he was getting at school lately, he also was looking toward the end of the season when he could get involved in thinking about other things. Every time he noticed the model airplane on his bookcase, he thought of how much he liked being around Donavon. Don did greet him once at school during the week and actually telephoned him Thursday night to see how he was holding up under the drills he knew Ryan was having the team do. "Don't be too much of a show-off at the pep rally tomorrow," he told Robbie.

Robbie was mostly in a fog all day Friday. He had trouble concentrating in his classes. In math class he was so out-of-it he never heard the teacher specifically call out his name. It was only when the kid next to him elbowed him that Robbie realized where he was. The class thought it was funny, but the teacher said, "We trust you will be more awake by tomorrow afternoon, Mr. Roberts."

The pep rally was wild. As Coach Ryan announced each player's name, he would step out of the line and take a bow. Some guys did it with a flourish, but Robbie just gave a wave.

The cheerleaders did a special routine for each of the starters. Robbie got a thrill out of hearing Jennifer O'Brian yell "Robbie Roberts, he's our man; if he can't do it, nobody can!"

That night practice went until six o'clock. Ryan's parting words to the team were "None of you guys have any homework to do tonight, so get a good night's sleep. I want to see all of you awake on the bus at two."

The Community College gym was larger than any the boys had played in during the regular season. It was a separate building on the sprawling campus. Robbie noted that the locker rooms were not as nice as those at Sparta Catholic, but they were carpeted. The shower room did not have any separate stalls, but it was bigger. The regional champions were given the 'home' locker area; Mountain Ridge was assigned the 'visitors' lockers.

A half hour later, when the Mountaineers took the floor, the gym erupted in loud cheering among a few 'boos.' Robbie thought that every seat was taken, but still managed to see who would be seated on the visitors' side, half up at the middle of the court. Sure enough, they were whistling, clapping, and yelling. Cee Jay was sitting next to his dad and his mother was opposite him. Three of his father's full-time employees sat just in front of them. Robbie was surprised to see that Barbie was also with the family, but sitting with her was Donavon Rice. *What the hell!* he thought. *Are they dating now?*

After the "Star Spangled Banner" was sung, the players for each team were introduced. The announcer made a point of introducing "Robbie Roberts, junior, playing center."

Looking in the direction of his family, he bowed and gave his now usual salute wave. Above all the cheers, Robbie thought he could make out Donavon's voice yelling the loudest.

Robbie couldn't let any of his fans down. He was determined to play his very best for them and his school in spite of his nervousness. He tried to concentrate on the game, but the first time he was fouled, he could actually feel his legs shaking. His hands were steady and his eyes were focused on the hoop. After he scored on both attempts his confidence grew and the nervousness was lost on playing.

At the end of the first quarter, Sparta Regional was leading 28 to Mountain Ridge's 22. Robbie had sunk for 12 points, Johnny Shaw got 6, and Roger Pucket got 4 at the line. By the end of the first half, Robbie was tired and sweating profusely. He merely made it into the locker room where he collapsed on the floor. The manager handed him a much-needed bottle of Gatorade and a towel.

Early in the second half it appeared that Sparta Regional would dominate the game. They were obviously better trained and handled the ball expertly. The Mountaineers never gave up, however, and continued to play as well as they could. Robbie was thankful that his team never resigned to the inevitable loss. With expert agility and speed, he continued to lead in scoring high.

A few minutes into the third quarter, Johnny Shaw was fouled and fell to the floor. Immediately Coach Ryan run out as the officials halted the game. The forward seemed to be in agony. The assistant coach kept the team away from those adults gathered around Shaw. Soon, a stretcher was called for. Word quickly spread that he had badly sprained his ankle in the fall and may have broken a bone. He would be sent to Newton Hospital for e-rays.

Jennifer O'Brian was seen breaking line with the cheerleaders to run over and kiss Johnny Shaw as he was carried off the court.

Ryan replaced Shaw with another senior player, Bob Walsh, who had not been on the court all season. Robbie had no idea how good Walsh was, but when the third quarter resumed, he and the replacement worked as a well-oiled machine and between them nearly closed the gap in the score. With only two-minutes left in the third, Ryan sent in two other second stringers. One was a senior, and a junior replaced Pucket.

Roger was back at the beginning of the fourth. Coach Ryan kept Walsh and Robbie in for the rest of the game. At every opportunity, the coach replaced a man, with different players who hadn't seen much action during the season to play the forward position. At the final buzzer, Sparta Regional won; the score was 68 to 60. Robbie was upset that his team lost the game, but was happy that once again he was the high scorer. He had made more baskets than any player on either side.

On his way to the locker room, Robbie was pulled aside by a man holding a microphone. Another man with a television camera was with him. "How does it feel to have scored more points than anyone on either team?" he asked, turning Robbie around to face the camera. "I understand that you are only a junior."

"Well, I, ah, ah, I would have preferred that Mountain Ridge would've won; but yeah, I'm glad that I played as well as I did. The entire team improved a heck of a lot during the second half of the season. Sparta played very well today, and they deserved the win, but, ah, they and all the other schools in the County should know that the Mountaineers are a young team and most of us will be back next year, and we'll be much better and more experienced."

"You've just heard what sounds like a challenge from junior star, Robbie Roberts. Thanks, Robbie, we'll be looking forward to seeing you next year." The reporter moved on to interview a Sparta Regional player.

In the locker room and shower, the Mountaineers were quiet and sad. A few seniors were wiping tears from their eyes. The mood was generally depressing, until Roger Pucket shouted: "Hey guys, fuck it! It's only a game! But my name's Pucket, and I love the game. So, eat your hearts out, seniors. I'll be back next year and you fuckers won't! And I'm gonna win that god-damn trophy!"

All the players started cheering and clapping. Even Coach Ryan, who had just entered the room was clapping.

The Coach congratulated his team for playing better than they ever had and far better than he had ever expected them to. He told them that the bus would take them back to their school now, but if they had a way of getting home from the college, they could stay to watch the second game to see who would be playing against Sparta Regional for the Championship game tomorrow.

Robbie knew that his father would be waiting for him in the gym, so he did not opt for the team bus. When Robbie met his dad on the bleachers, only Cee Jay was with him. "Your mom, took Barbie and Donavon home in her car. We'll go home with Cee Jay," Jamie said after hugging his son. Robbie was shocked when Cee Jay also gave him a bear hug and congratulated him on how well he played.

He was glad that Cee Jay was there. He was glad that Cee Jay had given him a hug. *Imagine! An English teacher hugging a junior so openly in the gym,* he thought. Then he wished that Don had stayed to hug him also. He didn't want to think why Don would have left with Barbie.

The three of them stayed to see the entire second game, which High Point won handily. The stage was set for the final game tomorrow between High Point and Sparta Regional. Robbie and Cee Jay predicted that Sparta Regional would win. Jamie felt that the Ogdensburg team had better control of the ball. They were still arguing when Cee Jay pulled into the Domino's Pizza parking lot. Jamie said, "Mom called in for two large pies, one with sausage—your favorite, and one with mushrooms," Jamie said as all three got out of Cee Jay's Chevy.

"I'm so hungry I'll probably eat the entire pie myself," Robbie said.

"Your mom said that she was also preparing a big salad," Cee Jay said.

Robbie assumed that Cee Jay would be joining them for this casual dinner, but was a bit annoyed to discover that Donavon Rice had also been invited to stay. *Probably Barbie's conniving,* he thought. He also wondered how Don would react to his teacher being in their house. Donavon went to Robbie and gave him a pat on the shoulder with one hand and shake with the other. Robbie thought this was very stiff and macho. He would have preferred a big, bear hug.

The salad and pizza was pretty much a help-yourself dinner on paper plates rather than formal plates. Melisa had a glass of wine, the two men each had two bottles of beer, and the teenagers finished a two litter of coke. The conversation revolved mostly around the two games and how well Robbie had played. At one point, Jamie said, "My son, the NBA player!"

After a while the conversation shifted to the project Barbie and Donavon were doing. This was Robbie's cue to inform everyone that he tired and said that he was going to go upstairs and to bed.

"I'll be going to the final game tomorrow, Robbie," Donavon said. "I plan on going with Bob Walsh in his car. I'm sure he'd like you to come with us. You guys played very well together today. Ryan should have used him more during the regular season."

Robbie hesitated. "Ah, I don't know. I'd feel kind'a funny being there, you know, ah being a loser. Besides isn't it obviously that Sparta will win the trophy again?"

"No, Robbie," Cee Jay said. "You shouldn't feel like a loser. You played very well and everyone knows that. I think you should go to that game. You'll be representing the spirit of the tournament."

"That's right, Dr. S," Donavon said. "Robbie, it would show that you are a good sport. So what do you say, Robbie, can Bob and I pick you up about two tomorrow?"

"Ah, I, ah. Dad, are you planning on going to the game?"

"No, son. I'll be at Cee Jay's all day tomorrow working on the plans for his basement renovation."

"Well, Okay, then, Don. I guess I'll tag along with you and Walsh."

"Great!" Donavon said as Robbie started up the stairs.

Chapter 13

Robbie awoke fully refreshed the next morning. He felt that he was finished with weeks of a hectic schedule between school and basketball. Today he could relax and watch the other guys; he was free of the tension and nervousness of the game. Now he could just sit back and enjoy. He also thought of Donavon and how great it would be to spend the afternoon in his presence. He wondered how close Bob Walsh and Don were. They both were seniors, but played different sports, and Bob didn't seem to be in the crowd that Don was usually surrounded by in the halls and the cafeteria. Donavon was a popular man and a great football player. Bob, on the other hand, was not that good on the basketball court, and generally seemed quiet and somewhat shy. Robbie hardly knew him before yesterday, even though they were on the same team. Walsh was not one of the loud mouth guys who told dirty jokes and mocked everyone. Robbie liked the opportunity to get to know him.

Before going to take his shower, Robbie stopped at his bookcase. He picked up the model B-29, and tuned it to examine it from all sides. He and Donavon had done a good job on it, and he really was happy that Don had given it to him to keep. He remembered the incident of cutting his finger. He smiled when he thought of Don as a "blood brother." He then realized that he had an erection.

When the two seniors arrived at the Roberts house, it was Barbie who answered the door. As Robbie was going down the stairs, he learned that Bob Walsh was also in their English class because they were discussing Bob's progress, or lack thereof, on his project. Robbie overheard Don tell Bob that he was happy to have Barbie as a partner and not Jennifer O'Brian, who was Bob's.

The ride to the Sussex County Community College was fun. Robbie was proud to be in Bob Walsh's car, listening to the good-natured jabs the guys were hitting him with. Bob told Robbie that when he got in the game yesterday, he was ready because he studied all the plays and Robbie's moves. He knew what to expect from the center. "Too bad Johnny Shaw didn't pay as much attention as you did," Donavon said. "Walsh told me last year that you would be very good on varsity, Robbie. Actually, it was Bob who told me to start watching the way you played."

"Really? Thanks, Bob. It's too bad you won't be at Mountain Ridge next year. We could'a made a good pair."

"Well, you and Roger Pucket will be good too. Say, did you hear Pucket in the locker room at the end of the game yesterday."

"Yeah," Robbie said. "That was classic Pucket."

"What was that?" Donavon inquired.

Bob Walsh relayed the story of how the senior guys came up with the 'Fuck it, Pucket! It's just a game!' story and how Roger reacted after yesterday's game. All three laughed to hear it.

"By the way, Roberts, I saw you on television on the news last night. They showed your interview after the game. You said the right words. Very good. Very diplomatic," Donavon said.

"Really," Robbie beamed. "You thought so?"

"Yeah, I saw it too," Bob remarked. "It was very sportsman like. And it gave a good message to the team and other schools for next year."

"Gee, thanks, guys," Robbie said.

Robbie had never thought of himself as a jock; but walking into the county college gym, he was elated to realize that maybe now he was. He thought of himself as part of that elite group he used to refer to as 'the jock posse.' He, a junior, was now hanging out with two seniors that he really liked. He thought that he would be filling their shoes next year. Many Mountain Ridge athletes were in the college gym. As they walked around to find seats, quite a few Mountaineers said 'Hi' and gave high-fives to Donavon and Bob, but many also congratulated Robbie for the great game he played. A guy from Sparta Ridge actually congratulated Robbie and told him that he gave a good interview after the game. Robbie enjoyed the adulation but tried to appear humble.

He deliberately sat between Donavon and Bob in the bleachers. Robbie wanted to be as close to Don as possible. He wanted to take in his Axe scent, to see Don up close, to feel his body close to his own, to occasionally feel his leg touch his own, to occasionally high-five and touch him with his own hand, and occasionally have Donavon pat him on his back.

Once during the first half, Robbie felt that Donavon pressed against his leg almost too hard and too deliberately. Robbie felt himself getting a hard-on, and immediately tried getting rid of it by turning to Bob. He had to get his mind off Don, but he couldn't quite stop asking himself *Why did Don do that? Why is my mind and my dick doing this? It's driving me crazy! It's way too homo, and I ain't a homo! I just like Donavon Rice. Can't one jock just 'like' another jock? Jocks are always touchy, feely, friendly with one another, right? ...Yeah, but do they get* boners *when they do?* Robbie thought.

During half-time the boys headed to the concession in the lobby. All three ordered cokes, but Don felt in the mood for

Nachos and cheese while Bob had a hot dog with chili. As they stood around, their school principal walked over to them. He greeted Donavon and Bob. Addressing Robbie, he said, "Robert, I got a call from the principal of Sparta Regional this morning consoling us on our loss, but he made special reference to how sportsmanlike you guys played. He was particularly impressed by your TV interview after the game. And, yes, we are all looking for an improved team next year." Turning back to Walsh, the principal said, "Bob, you and Robert were very good on the court. Too bad we didn't see more of the two of you together on the court during the regular season. Well, let's see Sparta do it again," he said leaving the trio.

Such praise from the principal, made Robbie even prouder. Both Don and Bob said that it was nice of the principal to come over and speak to them. All three appreciated it.

Before going back into the gym, Don offered to share the rest of his nachos with Robbie who gratefully accepted. The warm cheese with a touch of pimento was excellent, but on the third bite, some of the cheese dripped on Robbie's chin and his jacket. Donavon immediately took his own napkin and wiped around Robbie's mouth, chin, and jacket. He just smiled warmly at Robbie who was too shocked to react. Bob Walsh just looked on without commenting.

To no one's surprise Sparta Regional won the game. Robbie wished that it was he rather than the captain of the Sparta team who received the trophy, but he knew that he had another season of play to do just that. He felt sorry for the High Point players, most of whom would be leaving high school without ever touching the county trophy. He also knew that, if they even made it to the State Finals, Sparta Regional would be defeated by the Pirates of Seton Hall Prep or Atlantic City, unequivocally the best two teams in the state that year.

On the way home, Robbie asked Bob how long he and Donavon had known one another. "Forever," Bob replied. "We went to the same elementary school and we live just a few doors from one another."

"Walsh also goes to Saint Anne's Church," Donavon said. "His mother and mine are volunteers there. We both were Cub Scouts at Saint Anne's. Walsh helped me a lot with my Eagle Scout project."

"Oh, cool!" was all Robbie could think of to say, but the phrase 'blood brothers' came to mind.

Robbie was happy that he did take Cee Jay's advice and go with Donavon and Bob to the final game. When they got to his house, he almost didn't want the day to end. Getting out of the car, Donavon said to him, "I'll call you during the week, Robbie. Let's try to set up something for next weekend. I'd like to go with you and your dad to fly your remote in the park. Maybe Dr. Seton can come along too."

"Okay, I'll see what my father's schedule is like." Robbie said goodbye to Bob Walsh, who responded "See, ya, Robbie."

Walking up to his front door, Robbie wondered why Don added Cee Jay to their group-outing at the park with the remote plane. Bob Walsh did not react to Don's invitation adding Cee Jay. Robbie wondered how much Donavon had told Walsh about his dad's friendship with their teacher.

Chapter 14

"Hello, This is Jamie."

"Hi, Mr. Roberts. Donavon Rice here."

"What's happening, Don? Good to hear from you. I bet your calling for either Barbie or Robbie."

"Well, actually, I'm calling to talk to Robbie and you." He emphasized the word 'and.' Did Robbie ask you yet about Saturday?"

"Saturday? No, he didn't say anything about Saturday to me. What's happening on Saturday that I should know about?"

"Well, on Sunday after the game, I asked Robbie to ask you if you guys would like to go to the park on Saturday to fly Robbie's remote air plane. This is only Wednesday. Maybe Robbie was going to ask you later. I talked to Dr. Seton about it in school this morning, and he said he would enjoy an afternoon in the park with us, but that I better check with you first. So, can you, sir?"

"Sure, it sounds good to me, if the weather is not too cold, too windy or too rainy. I'm surprised Robbie hasn't mentioned it to me, though. Flying the remote is always fun for us, and having you and Cee Jay along this time will make it even more fun. Robbie is upstairs doing homework right now. I'll talk to him and have him call you within an hour. He does have your number, doesn't he?"

"Thanks Mr. Roberts. I'm looking forward to it. See you on Saturday then. Hopefully."

"Goodbye, Don. Thanks for calling."

Putting the phone down, Jamie turned to his wife who was sitting in their living room with him. "That's strange," he said with a puzzled facial expression.

"What's strange, dear?" Melissa sked.

"Donavon Rice wanted to know if Cee Jay, Robbie, and I are going to the park on Saturday to fly Robbie's remote. He said that he asked Robbie to ask me about it on Sunday. Normally, Robbie would be bouncing all over me to go, but he hasn't mentioned a word about it this time. Has he said anything about it to you, honey?"

"mmm. No, he hasn't said anything to me either."

"I better go up and talk to him. It's not like Robbie to forget something like this."

Upstairs, Jamie knocked on his son's door.

"Yeah. Come on in," Robbie responded. Seeing it was his father, he smiled broadly.

"What's up, dad?"

"Robbie, I just got off the phone with Donavon Rice. He was asking me about flying your remote in the park with Cee Jay on Saturday. He said that he asked you to check with me on Sunday. I had to tell him that you never mentioned it. I thought you would be excited about flying the remote; you usually are begging me to go to the park. I was wondering if something was wrong, son. Why you haven't asked me yet, I mean. You know I like flying your model almost as much as you do, Robbie."

Robbie was silent for a moment. "Yes, dad I do like flying the plane with you." He accented the 'you.' "But with Cee Jay and Donavon joining in, I'm not too sure I'd like that. I deliberately didn't ask you. I was hoping that Don would forget about it, and if he did, I was going to tell him that you couldn't make it."

"And, what about Cee Jay."

"Don said he wanted him to join us."

"So? What's wrong with that? You like Cee Jay, don't you, son?"

"Yes, but playing with my models, is something just between you and me."

"Robbie, Cee Jay is part of my life now. You know that we love one another and want to be together, doing things together. I know that Cee Jay is happy to have you as part of his extended family. I thought you were accepting this fact, son."

"Well, yeah, but now there also seems to be Donavon."

"I like Don, and I thought you did too. Cee Jay thinks he is a good guy too."

"Dad, don't you think that Don may be getting ideas about you and Cee Jay?"

"Is that it? Do you think that Don may suspect that we are lovers?"

"Hell, yes! And what if he starts blabbering that all over?"

"If he really is a friend, Robbie, he wouldn't spread any bad rumors. Whatever Donavon may suspect about us, is his own right to think; but I do not think he is the type of person to spread humors. If some day he actually asks you, me, or Cee Jay, if we are lovers, I know that neither I nor Cee Jay would deny it. We are not about to deny who we are to him or anyone else for that matter. Donavon seems like a mature guy who can understand and handle the truth."

"Yeah, but..."

"But, nothing, young man. You like Donavon, and Cee Jay and I think that he likes you too. So, get over it! If we're not afraid of it, neither should you." Jamie saw tears beginning to well in Robbie's eyes. "What's wrong, Robbie?"

"Yeah, I like Donavon." He paused. Sobbing, he said, "But I don't want him to come between you and me. We've always gone flying. Just you and me."

Jamie put his arms around Robbie. "I know, Robbie. Flying your models was our special thing, and probably always will be; but now you have a good friend and so do I. It's nice to share special times with special people in our lives. I guess in a way it helps us to grow.; but sometime that growth is hard. Change is part of life. Do you realize that last Sunday was the first time I didn't go with you to a basketball game? That was sad for me. I knew you had to go with Donavon. In a way you were leaving me, but I knew you needed to be with friends. That didn't mean that your old man loved you any less. Yeah, I would have liked to go to that game with you, but you needed the space to be with your friend. I know that at first you didn't want to go to the final game, but when Cee Jay and Donavon said you should go, you agreed. I bet you had a good time too. Didn't you? "

Wiping tears from his face, Robbie said, "Yeah, I did like being with Don and Bob."

"Parents hate when their kids start wanting to be with friends more than them, but that's the way things are. You have no idea how your mother and I are dreading to see Barbie leave home to go to college in just a few months. We're going to lose our little girl to a whole new world for her. And you too, may be going away from us in less than two years. So we all have to start the separation process, I guess." Jamie felt his own eyes beginning to tear.

"It's called 'change', Robbie. We all change, but we need to embrace it, not run away from it."

There was silence between the father and son. Jamie finally kissed Robbie on his forehead and said, "Now, I want you to go downstairs, call Donavon, and tell him that the three of us will pick him up at 1:30 at his house on Saturday."

On Saturday Jamie and Robbie went to the office and took the air plane off the chains that held it to the ceiling.

"Don really wants to see this thing fly, dad."

"And isn't it great that you can share your own fun with him? ...Like you did skiing at the Manor in December?"

"Yeah, I like doing things with Don.

"Good!" Jamie was pensive and had to hold back a tear. "Now let's get this thing in the Ram. You have to sit in the bed to hold it down. Did you put the controller in the cab? Extra batteries? We'll pick Cee Jay up before going to Don's house. You and Don will have to sit in the bed until we get to the park."

It was a beautiful first day of spring. This year there had been no hint of the usual St. Patrick's Day light snow fall New Jersey usually experienced. All four men agreed that it was a perfect day-crisp and clean—for remotely flying a model air plane. Jamie parked his pick -up along the road as close to the gazebo as possible. Robbie loved this area of the county park. Cherry blossom trees, that were just beginning to bloom, surrounded the gazebo. In front of the band stand was a paved area with some benches where handicapped people could sit as well as others who didn't bring their lawn chairs to hear the band concerts. The paved area was smooth and served as a run way for the model.

Robbie sat on one of the benches, and Donavon kept his eyes on the controller. Cee Jay watched as Jamie positioned the plane for take-off. Robbie was proud that he was giving flight instructions to the senior boy. Cee Jay was on his hands and knees as was Jamie. Their 'toy' was four feet long and had a six-foot wing span.

On Jamie's command, Robbie pressed the button to start the propeller. "Now check the flaps!" As Robbie worked on the controller, the plane shook a little. "Okay, let her run, Robbie."

The model started moving straight ahead on the paving, picking up speed as Robbie raised the throttle. Robbie showed Don how to get the plane in the air. When it was about fifty feet in the air and clear of the trees, Robbie radioed a wide turn to the right. He showed Donavan how to make it turn right and left, fly lower or higher. After flying for about ten minutes, Robbie sent the signals to begin a gentle descent to where Jamie and Cee Jay were now standing. The teacher who was filming the entire flight now focused in on Donavon and Robbie and then as the plane bounced on the pavement, Jamie, stuck his tongue out and shook his head. "The eagle has landed!" he shouted. "Good, job, Captain Roberts."

When the engine stopped, Robbie began a review and gave additional instructions to Don. "I'll act as co-pilot for your first flight," he told Don. "Don't do anything crazy. I want my DC-3 to return in one piece."

"Hey, isn't that the kind of advice I gave you skiing?"

"Yes, and I obeyed your orders. Now, you obey mine."

"I, I, Captain."

Robbie handed the controller to his partner. Donavon followed the same flight plan that Robbie had. He was thrilled by the plane's response to the slightest movement of his hand. Robbie's eyes darted from Donavon's manipulations at the controller and the plane. Almost flawlessly, Don brought the plane to the ground. Jamie and Cee Jay clapped when the engine was turned off.

"And now, gentlemen," Jamie said, "a brief lesson on aerodynamics and engineering. Gather round now."

"Good," Cee Jay said. "I have no idea how a plane gets up in the air." Both the senior student and teacher sat on the grass as Jamie gave a lesson on lift and velocity. Robbie lectured on the design and parts of the model. Jamie asked Don to explain the radio controls on the controller to Cee Jay. "Here's where the student becomes the teacher, and the teacher the student," Jamie said.

"And in this case, dad and I will assure that Don has learned his lessons well."

"Okay, Dr. S. Gladly would he learn and gladly would he teach."

Cee Jay smiled, "I'm glad someone was paying attention during my classes on Chaucer. Very good." Turning to Jamie he said, "That's from *Canterbury Tales*."

Jamie looked at Robbie. "More specifically, son, it's from the "The Prologue."

Donavon laughed. "Very good, Mr. Roberts."

In his best southern-belle accent, Cee Jay said, "Ma dear Mista Roberts, you do amaze me with your knowledge of lit-er-a-ture. Imagine! A handsome gentleman who knows about saawws and nails, an' hammers an' such, also knows Mista Geoffrey Chaucer."

Everyone laughed. "By the way, Dr. S, speaking of saws and hammers, how is your basement renovation coming along?" Donavon asked.

"What? Oh, the basement renovation? That's…How did you know about the basement renovation?

"Last week, Mr. Roberts said that he was going to your house to work on your basement."

"Donavon, I'm sure Jamie, Mr. Jerimiah Roberts, of the Roberts Construction Company, would love to have my money for a renovation project, but the truth of the matter is that 'basement renovation' is really code for: 'hang out at Dr. Seton's house.'"

Donavon's "Oh!" was more of a question.

Jamie quickly explained. "I've been telling your teacher for months that he has a perfectly good space in his cellar for a terrific man cave. Not only would it be a good place to hang out, entertain, give parties, etc. but the investment would greatly increase the value of his house. Finished basements are in great demand now."

"Wow! A man cave! I like that, Dr. S. ...Hey, maybe Robbie and I can come to some of your wild bachelor parties."

"Don't even think of it, young man," Cee Jay said.

"Don, I keep telling him that I'll charge minimum for labor and I get materials wholesale. I'd even do the drawings and get all the permits free. You should see the potential he has."

"I'd like that," Donavon said. "You know, I'm interested in engineering and architecture. If I saw your basement, Dr. S, I might be able to give you and Mr. Roberts some ideas."

"Oh, now I see what's happening here," Cee Jay said jokingly. "You two are in cahoots for a project renovating my basement. How much commission do you get, Mr. Rice?"

"Seriously, on the way home today, let's stop at your place and show Don your house. He may be able to convince you of the possibilities," Jamie said.

"Okay, I'll let him see my basement. I guess that's the only way I'll get to fly the Roberts' air plane." Taking the controller, he said, "Gentlemen, you will now be astounded by the world-famous World War II flying ace, Wolfgang Von Seton's aeronautical skills."

Jay Cee did have perfect control of flying the DC-3 model. With Jamie's help, he navigated a figure 8 and several loops, logging in about fifteen minutes in the air. Donavon seemed impressed by how adroit his teacher was in handling the plane. He also noticed how handsome he looked in a soft brown leather vest over a plaid flannel shirt and Gloria Vanderbilt jeans that fit snuggly to his body and outlined a substantial crotch and firm-looking ass. *No wonder all the girls at school go gaga over this guy*, he thought. *He's got class! Robbie's dad is good looking, too. No wonder they're friends*. Donavon thought that it was hard to tell which of the two men he liked more. Jamie seemed to be more fun, but Dr. S definitely, he thought, was better looking. His friend, Robbie, on the other hand, didn't take fashion lessons from either of the two adults. Don wondered what Robbie would look like in something other than the baggy cargo pants and loose-fitting tee shirts he always wore. *But Robbie definitely is cuter*, he concluded.

Robbie, on the other hand, was concentrating only on Donavon. He admired how muscular the quarterback was. He was strikingly handsome wearing tight jeans and a light bomber jacket. He needed a shave, but Robbie thought that the five o'clock shadow made him look even sexier. Robbie thought that someday he might ask Don if he could run his hands through his full, wavy light brown hair. *I'd probably come in my pants, if that ever happened*, he thought. *No wonder all the girls at school think he's hot. God, I think he's hot! And I ain't gay!... or am I?...Straight guys don't think about guys the way I think about Donavon. Do they?*

It was now Jamie's turn to fly the air plane. Robbie knew that this would be the best part of the day. He loved the way his dad maneuvered the plane in the sky. He knew his dad was good, but Donavon and Cee Jay were amazed. At one point, he flew the plane low enough to buzz Cee Jay. At another time he seemed to be aiming it straight at Donavon but brought the nose straight up in front of him. Even Robbie didn't know how to do this without stalling.

Cee Jay continued to film the whole thing. *If I ever show this film to the boys, I'll have to edit out my close-ups of Jamie's face and his amazing package,* he thought.

Jamie brought the plane into a perfect landing. The four men sat in a circle around the model. They talked about how good the weather was for flying. "I'm surprised there's no one in the park with a kite today," Don said. "I used to love to fly a kite, but I haven't done that in years. Not since my dad died."

"Hey, let's do that soon," Jamie said. "The four of us! I haven't flown a kite since Robbie was a baby. As a youngster, Robbie was always into air planes."

"I'm going to start taking flying lessons as soon as I can. Dad says there's a training school down in Morristown that he would take me to."

"Don't you want to learn to drive a car first?" Don asked.

"I suppose, but I want to feel flying, moving about freely in the air and seeing the ground below. I actually think I'd prefer to fly over driving a car."

"Well, I'll be happy when I get a car in about three months," Donavon said.

The two boys sat in the bed of Jamie's pick up again on the way home. Donavon was surprised that Jamie didn't take him home first since he lived closest to the park. "Dad's probably taking you to see Dr. S's basement before taking you home," Robbie explained.

"Oh, yeah. The man cave thing. Cool!" Donavon responded.

Crackers was at the window, then the door, and back to the window. The golden retriever was barking well before the pick-up came to a stop in front of Cee Jay's garage door. He had been waiting for his master's return. As soon as Cee Jay opened the door, the dog was out the door jumping up and wildly wagging his tail. Cee Jay got on his knees to rub his pet. "Good boy! Did you miss me, Crackers? I bet you would have loved running in the park with us. Wouldn't you have, boy?"

After the greeting from his master, the dog jumped onto Jamie who also rubbed him.

"I've brought you two new friends, Crackers, meet Don and Robbie."

The dog went to Robbie's feet and sniffed and then to Don and did the same. Don got down on his knees to hug the pet who in turn began smearing his tongue over Don's face. Don started laughing, "Robbie, get this mad dog off me. I think he is in love with me."

"Crackers! Settle down." Cee jay interrupted the dog's kisses. "He's very happy to meet you, Donavon. I should have warned you how overly friendly he can be. Come on in guys."

Cee Jay ushered Jamie and the two teenagers into his living room. Take a seat while I get Crackers some water and take him out to the backyard. Jamie why don't you get some sodas out of the refrigerator?"

Momentarily, Robbie and Donavon were left alone in the living room. Looking around the room, Don said, "Dr. S has a nice place here. I've never been in a teacher's house before. This is a first for me. Have you been here before?"

"Just once. The day we came back from skiing in the Poconos. He took me all through it that day. My dad comes here quite often. Dr. S visits our house a lot too."

"Cool! I'm anxious to see the basement," Donavon said as Jamie reentered the room with four bottles of soda. "All I could find was Mountain Dew. Cee Jay loves this stuff. Tastes like and looks like piss to me," Jaime said. "But beggars can't be choosy, I guess." He sank into the leather sofa opposite the fireplace.

Cee Jay entered the room. "Well, are you guys ready to explore my dungeon?"

"Dungeon?" Robbie echoed.

"Don't give my boy any ideas of whips and chains and racks, Cee Jay."

"Okay. Shall we explore my dark and dank areas?"

"Hey, let's make your man cave into a bat cave," Don said. "By day he is a mild-mannered teacher, but at night he is a crime fighter and from his bat cave he emerges as 'Bat Man' with his trusted partner, 'Bat Boy.' Robbie, you can be Robin, 'Bat Boy.' You'd look cool in tight green underwear and a cape, Robbie."

"Jamie, this boy is spending too much time around you. Your kooky ideas are rubbing off on him."

"To the bat cave, then," Jamie led the guys to the cellar.

Donavon was pleased to see how big the basement was. "Wow, you could have a regular, nine foot ceiling down here. I don't see any evidence of water. That's good. Many basements have dampness which can cause mold."

"Okay, Don, do your thing. What would you do with this space?" Jamie asked.

Donavon walked around the open basement for a while before speaking. "Mr. Roberts is right, Dr. S. You do have great possibilities here. First, the ceilings are high, so even tall people like us won't have to bend down or even brush their heads on the ceiling. The stairs coming down are almost dead center which gives you full use of the entire area. Your electric panel is on this wall so you can easily run wires for recessed lighting in this area and put in the necessary outlets on all four walls. I see you already have a washer and dryer here, so you have the 220 wiring necessary for baseboard heaters." He spread his hands to demonstrate what he saying.

"This whole area could be one large entertainment area. Picture a heavy, rustic bar over here. You have a gas furnace, so you can easily have a gas fireplace with ceramic logs in this corner to make the room have a nice cozy feel while you have a glass of wine from the bar. I would suggest you divide the area behind the stairs into three separate rooms, the two on either side should open to the bar area on one side and the fireplace area over here. Mr. Roberts may have to raise the floor over here to install a half bath. If you do much entertaining down here you will want to have at least a toilet and sink down here, but with the height of the ceiling you would still have about seven feet."

Jaime, who had been considering everything Donavon was saying with nods of his head and an occasion "mmm" now said, "Cee jay, this kid is a genius. Listen to him."

"Yes, he is picturing it rather clearly for me," Cee Jay responded. "Go on, Don."

"You would want to close off the furnace and laundry areas; make it a separate room. Have storage closets or shelves over here to fill the gap where the half bath would be. And now for the piece d' resistance of the floor plan. In this big area you could have a two tier home theater. I saw one in a model home that was just built in Ogdensburg and it was a real selling point for the people going through the house. Imagine a full wall screen there with the video projector in the ceiling. You can have six or eight plush chairs in the room."

"That really sounds expensive, Don. Great, but maybe more than I could afford."

"Think big, Dr. S! It may not be that expensive. I hear Mountain Ridge is replacing some of the seats in the auditorium this summer. You might be able to get some at auction at a very low price." Donavon looked for some reaction from the three men. Jamie and Cee Jay were deep in thought. Robbie seemed to be beaming with pride at how creative and knowledgeable about construction his friend was.

Donavon continued. "Imagine this great room-slash bar area—having faux beams in the ceiling, and wainscoting and chair railing on the three side walls. You can cover those three windows with a decorative cellophane to create a stained glass look and privacy. Oh, and let's not forget, you have this area for a pool table and dart board."

Jamie went to him and put his arm around Don's shoulder. "This kid is going to make a great architect someday. I might even make him a partner in an architectural and construction company."

"If you would like me to draw up some illustrations and write out some specs, Dr. S, I'd be happy to do that and I'd make a copy for Mr. Roberts so he could price the whole project out. With his getting materials for you at wholesale and doing some of the work as a labor of love, I'm roughly guessing you would be coming in under five thousand. Wouldn't you agree, Mr. Roberts?"

"That seems about right, but I would have to sit down and itemize all the specs before giving a more precise estimate for the job. Let's work on it, Don. If you give me your illustrations and plans by next week I'll have a good estimate for you, Cee Jay, the following week. It's possible we could christen your man cave by having a graduation party for Donavon and Barbie here. But only if you promise to play the piano and let me and Melissa do karaoke."

"As Donavon was describing his thoughts, it reminded me of La Bar, Jamie."

"Ah, La Bar!...I wonder if it's still there."

"What's La Bar?" Donavon asked.

"Oh, it's some dive down in Greenwich Village, New York, where Cee Jay and I used to hang out."

Seemingly as though on cue, and without hesitation, Jamie started to sing:

> *Once upon a time there was a tavern*
> *Where we used to raise a glass or two*
> *Remember how we laughed away the hours*
> *And think of all the great things we would do.*

The two teenagers were aghast and then totally stunned when Cee Jay began singing along.

> *Those were the days my friend*
> *We thought they'd never end*
> *We'd sing and dance forever and a day*
> *We'd live the life we choose*
> *We'd fight and never lose*
> *For we were young and sure to have our way.*

Jamie and Cee Jay locked arms in front of the boys. Both men started swaying to the music.

Then the busy years went rushing by us
We lost our starry notions on the way
If by chance I'd see you in the tavern
We'd smile at one another and we'd say.

"Come on now boys," Jamie said. "Sing along. Follow us."
Donavon immediately picked up the chorus. By the second line,
following Don's cue, Robbie also started singing along.

Those were the days my friend
We thought they'd never end
We'd sing and dance forever and a day
We'd live the life we choose
We'd fight and never lose
Those were the days; oh, yes those were the days.

When their impromptu singing ended, the boys clapped. All
four chuckled, and they headed back up-stairs. Neither Robbie
nor Donavon said anything, but both teenagers were aware
that Cee Jay and Jamie still had their arms around one another.
They sensed—but could not articulate—a feeling between the
two adults.

Chapter 15

IT RAINED ALMOST EVERY day the following week; and when it wasn't raining, the skies were threatening. It was cold and damp, and these conditions didn't help Robbie's mood. He missed the adrenal rush of the basketball season. He also missed the guys on his team, who seemed to disappear into the mainstream. Roger Pucket, his junior friend, teammate, and regular lunch buddy developed a bad cold and was kept out of school. Worst of all, Robbie had the impression that Donavon was deliberately not even noticing him at school. Once, however, when they passed in the halls, Donavon did say "What's up, Roberts?" and kept walking. They had a really good time in the park on Saturday, and now Donavon acted like a stranger.

It was pouring on Friday evening when Donavon called. He asked Melissa, who answered the phone, if he could speak with Mr. Roberts. Don called to tell Jamie that he had finished the illustrations, floor plans, and specs for Cee Jay's basement man cave. He wanted to know if he could drop them off at the construction office on Saturday. Jamie volunteered to drop by at Donavon's house to get them, but Don said that it might be easier if he just bicycled to the office. "My wife, Robbie and I usually go to the office for a few hours every Saturday; so, if you want to, pedal on over. I hope it stops raining by then. I'm anxious to see what you came up with."

The day was as beautiful as last Saturday. Donavon arrived at the J. Roberts Construction and Contracting Company at 10:00. Jamie greeted him warmly as did Melissa and Robbie. The two boys talked a little about Donavon's bike; Robbie asked if Don thought that seven speeds were really necessary for cruising around their town. Jamie then ushered him down a hall and into his office.

"Don is a very nice young man," Melissa said. "Barbie says he is very good to work with on their English project. She also said that he is very serious, but can be very funny too. Between you and me, Robbie, I think your sister has a crush on your friend."

"Really? You think so?"

"Oh, I can tell. But I'm not surprised. Donavon is a good looking young man." She emphasized 'is' and winked. "In many ways he reminds me of your father when he was Don's age. Your father could charm the devil in those days. He certainly swept me off my feet. Yep, your dad was my first and only love. Still is."

"What about Cee Jay, though?" Robbie asked.

"Robbie, your father has a great capacity for love. He needs Cee Jay. Actually, I think they both need each other. Cee Jay is a good man and your father loves him. That's good enough for me. I learned to share his love a long time ago, even before your sister and you came into our lives. I really am happy that he and Cee Jay were able to reconnect after so many years. You know, son, I believe that there would be more happy households and fewer divorces if there were more friends like Cee Jay and my husband in this world. But that just may be my opinion. I guess you might call me 'unconventional.' I'm a product of the 1960's. But enough about me. How are you handling the relationship between your father and Cee Jay?"

"Mom, can you really accept that gay stuff?" Robbie blurted.

"What do you mean by 'gay stuff', Robbie?"

"You know, sex."

"Well, sex is an expression of love. When you love someone, you want to give that person pleasure. You want to be as close as possible. You want to feel that your body and your loved one kind of melt. Touching, kissing, all of that. Is that what you mean by sex?"

"Yeah, but really, mom, two guys doing it. Isn't that disgusting to you?"

"No, Robbie, it isn't disgusting at all. God made us to have different feelings. Love is an emotion and physically connecting our bodies to another human being—male or female—is the greatest emotion there is. Making love should never be considered dirty or disgusting. Rape is disgusting. I don't personally approve of indiscriminate sex just for a quick, pleasurable release. I think group sex is morally wrong, but sex between two people who really care for one another is a beautiful thing, a God-given thing."

"Every time I think of Cee Jay and dad having sex, I get upset."

Melissa paused to carefully frame her son's sentiment. "Why, Robert Roberts, I am shocked to hear you dwell on such things. Do you think about your father and me making love also? ... We do, you know."

"Of course not!"

"Well, that's good to know, because our intimacies are none of your business. And neither should you think about any sex acts between your father and Cee Jay or any other people for that matter. Cee Jay is a teacher, he's human, and humans have sex. Please don't tell me you think about Miss Caulfield, your math teacher, having sex with her boyfriend."

"mmm. I'm beginning to see your point, mom, but isn't gay sex sinful?"

"I guess we have to examine what a sin is. Yes, some churches do think sex between two men is a sin. But they also condemn sex between a man and a woman who are not lawfully married. Our own religion, Catholicism, preaches that you should only have sex when you deliberately want to conceive a child, and bans the use of birth control except for the so-called rhythm method, which I personally feel reduces human beings to nothing more than reproductive machines. Fundamental religious beliefs have dictated attitudes toward human sexual behavior for centuries. Do you know that some religions and societies actually encourage polygamy? Historians say that in some ancient cultures homosexual love was greater than that between a man and woman. A wife was there just to produce off-spring to be heirs. Those attitudes are often imbedded in different cultures, but civilizations and cultures do change. The idea of a man having a mistress is practically a sign of his wealth in our country…Why, William Randolph Hurst actually kept a mistress in the same house with his wife.

"I think that our own society is waking up to the fact that homosexuality exists, and always will, among men and women as well. Some people are born with the genitalia of one sex but the mind and spirit of another. These people are transgenders. That's a good term to use. I think 'lesbian' to describe a woman who loves other women is good also. The words I don't like are 'gay' and 'faggot.' They are not only harmful but misleading. They imply effeminacy or subservience or worse yet, silliness and artificiality. A small number of homosexuals may be 'gay' but most homosexuals are anything but. I assure you, Robbie, your father is bi-sexual and Cee Jay is homosexual. The term 'gay' is 100% wrong for either man."

There was a moment of silence. "Thanks for having this discussion with me, mom. I guess I need to do more thinking and research on the subject. And stop listening to the jerks at school who don't really do any research or thinking."

"Good. I'm glad, too. But one other thing, Robbie. As you mature, you should grow to be the person God intended you to be. You should follow your own natural instincts. Whatever your inclinations may be, don't be afraid to embrace them." Melissa smiled and jokingly added, "God! I hope that I don't obsess on what you might be doing in bed on your wedding night, or how you go about making me a grandmother."

Donavan and Jamie walked back into the main room. "Well, have you two planned Cee Jay's man cave?" Melissa asked.

"I'm very impressed at what Don has done. He has some great ideas and his drawings and specifications are presented very well. I'll go over the pricing for Cee Jay this afternoon and give the bid to him later today. Again, great job, Don?" He and Donavon shook hands.

"Thanks Mr. Roberts. I hope Dr. Seton likes the plans also." Before leaving, Don turned to Robbie. "Say it's such a beautiful day. Why don't the two of us do some bicycling. Maybe go to the park."

"Yeah, I'd like that!" Robbie exclaimed. "Dad, mom, is it okay with you?

"Sure," both parents said simultaneously. "We're just about finished here?" Melissa said. "So, why don't we put Don's bike in the back of the pick-up and we can get Robbie's bike at home and you guys can go together from there."

"That sounds like a plan," Donavon said.

As soon as they got home, Robbie got his own bicycle from the garage and unloaded Don's bike from the pick-up. "How about I make a few sandwiches for you guys to take to the park? It's warm enough for a little picnic," Melissa said.

Both boys agreed that taking some food to the park was a great idea. Melissa made ham and cheese sandwiches with tomato and lettuce. She also packed Sunny Delight bottles, and several Twinkies for them.

Bicycling with Donavon made Robbie happy. On the way to the park, they joked and cut one another off several times. Robbie challenged Donavon to race down one street, Donavon won. He made circles waiting for Robbie to catch up. The senior boy's 'victory dance' included his riding ahead with both arms raised high and yelling "Put some metal to the pedal, slow poke."

The boys dropped their bikes on the pavement in front of the gazebo band shell. They decided to have their lunch on the steps. "It was really nice of your mom to make us a lunch, Roberts."

"Don, why do you always call me by my last name?"

"I don't know, Roberts. Maybe because I just call a lot of people by their last names. I don't think I've ever called Walsh by any other name. It is Bob, isn't it? Bob Walsh. Yeah, that's Walsh's name, isn't it? He's never asked why I don't refer to him as Bob or Robert, though. I know that's your name, too. Robert, I mean. Robert Roberts…Odd. Why does everyone call you Robbie, not Robert or Bob?"

"I don't know. I guess it's because my dad's real name is Jeremiah, but everyone calls him Jamie. So, it kind'a rimes. Jamie and Robbie, get it?"

"If I had a kid, I'd never call him Jamie or Robbie."

"Why not?"

"It sounds like a kid's name, that's why. Last year in English we studied **Death of a Salesman**. In that play the main character's name is Willy Loman. Arthur Miller, who wrote the play, deliberately used Willy because the guy never really grew up. You know, matured. He thought and acted like a kid, even though he was an old man. Miller also named him Loman because he was just that, a low man on a socio-economic level. Great use of symbolism, wouldn't you say."

"So, do you think of me as an immature kid?" Robbie asked.

"Hell, no. I just think of you as a jerk off!" Don said poking Robbie with his elbow. "No, I'm just joshing with you, Roberts. I guess I never gave it much thought before. I think it's macho to call guys by their last names. I'd never refer to a girl that way though. I can't think of calling your sister Barbie, 'Roberts.' It's a guy thing with me." He put his arm around Robbie and drew him closer. "Now that I think about it, Robbie is cute...And you are cute. I'll try calling you Robbie from now on. Only because you are so damn cute." He lovingly shook the younger boy's shoulder.

Finishing his sandwich and grabbing for a Twinkie, Robbie said, "May I ask you another question, Don?"

"Sure, Robbie, you can ask me anything. Unless, of course, it's not about how babies are made. You'd have to ask your dad about that."

Robbie smiled. "No, dad gave me the 'talk' a long time ago."

"Good. Because my father—er, step-father—never told me about sex. Mom did, a little; but most of what I know about sex, I learn from Walsh and company. The sex ed they teach at Mountain Ridge is a joke." He paused. "So what's on your mind, young man?"

"Well, why do you ignore me at school? When we met at the Manor Lodge in December, you were real friendly. You're friendly whenever we're together, but at school you hardly recognize me. Why?"

"Probably because I seldom, if ever, do see you at school. I know that we have the same lunch period, but I'm usually in the café with Walsh and the same group of guys every day. I know that you usually eat with Roger Pucket and some other juniors and the same girl."

"You must mean Judy Ferrero. Yeah, she follows Roger around like a puppy dog all the time. I don't think Roger even likes her that much."

"Oh, I thought she was your girlfriend."

"You got to be kidding! Judy Ferrero and me? No way! I don't have a girlfriend." Robbie paused. "Not yet, at any rate."

"Neither do I," Don said. "Not yet. I go out with a lot of girls, but that really doesn't mean any of them are my girlfriends. Don't tell anyone, Robbie, but I'm still a virgin."

"Oh." Both boys stopped talking momentarily.

"You know, you could always join Walsh and me at our lunch table."

"No," Robbie said. "That might be a bit awkward."

"I know. I'd feel that same way going over to you and Roger and what's her name…Judy Ferrero. Have you ever noticed how the kids at Mountain Ridge all seem to segregate themselves? Everyone says that jocks hang around one another. But why is it that the black kids always sit in the same area; the goths are always at the tables by the door; the nerds are close to the teachers' dining room; the butch girls and fag boys are close to the lunch line; and the special ed class is always in the corner. No one tells you where to sit in the cafeteria, but kids just seem to find their own groups." Don paused.

"If you see me in the halls, I'm not ignoring you, Robbie. I'm usually running from a class at one end of the building to another or maybe in a deep conversation with someone from one of my classes. I'm sorry if I may have hurt your feelings, Robbie; but believe me, I don't want to ignore you. I like you too much not to give you notice. And I'm not limiting my watching you to just on the basketball court. I've been—shall we say, a fan?—of yours for over a year. That's why I was so glad to meet you in the Poconos."

After a moment, Donavon said, "Enough of this bull shit. I have to be at my Micky D's job by six o'clock...Now, to the bat bikes!"""

Getting up, Robbie was not aware of having a hard on, but he did feel a sticky seepage in his briefs.

Chapter 16

THE FOOTBALL SEASON WAS over. The basketball season was over. Graduation was still a long way off for the seniors. A couple of girls were absent because of pregnancies; a couple of boys quit school to get jobs; one joined the marines. Those who were going to college had sent in their applications a month ago and were now waiting for acceptance notices. Most of the seniors had the annual condition known as 'senioritis.' The juniors were showing those familiar ostentatious signs of affection. To fill in the gap before the usual student council and class elections and the senior class trip, there seemed to be only one thing to concentrate on; and Mountain Ridge High School was in preparation for its annual gala: The Prom. The prom theme—"Broadway Melody"—had been voted on a few weeks ago. Ironically, it was Barbie Roberts who suggested the title, and while all the girls and guys were vying for who would be asked and by whom and who would be chosen the king and queen of the event, Barbie herself was still not asked by any of the eligible young studs in the senior class. Only those juniors who would be escorted by seniors could attend.

Barbie and the other members of "the" committee had decided on having a dinner-dance affair at Mayfair Farms Country Club in Millburn. It was Jennifer O'Brian who convinced the cheerleaders to select her suggestion for the combo to provide the music. The group consisted of four music majors from Montclair State who not only submitted the lowest of the three bids, but it was later learned that Johnny Shaw's older brother was their singer/band leader. Because they were just a few years older, the group it was said, knew all the tunes "today's" teens wanted to hear.

Committees were also formed for selling the tickets, getting the favors, choosing a professional photographer, making a program, and making the seating charts and selecting the menu. In addition to the principal and his wife, Dr. Charles Seton and Dr. Marilyn Jorgensen of the language department would be the faculty chaperones. The art department supplied the materials for the cheerleaders to make posters advertising the big affair. The excitement seemed to exponentially increase each day as the halls and cafeteria were covered by prom announcements. All the seniors felt that not only would "Broadway Melodies" be the social event of the year, but would be one that future classes would try to emulate.

While Barbie was busy planning for the prom, she was getting worried that with only two weeks left before it, she still had not been asked. Her brother, Robbie, could not care about the fuss. He and some other juniors had even begun ridiculing the upper classmen for their excessive enthusiasm for this one night of great pomp and expense. At home Robbie even jokingly asked Barbie to be his date for the prom.

Going downstairs for breakfast on Saturday morning, Robbie overheard his mother and Barbie talking excitedly about the prom. His mother said, "Oh, honey I'm so happy for you. We'll go out this afternoon and get your prom gown."

"Good morning, ladies," Robbie cheerfully said entering the kitchen. "What's this I over-heard just now? Barbie paid some nerd to take her to the prom? Who's the sucker, sis?"

"For your information, little brother, Donavon Rice has asked me to be his date."

"What?" Robbie was truly stunned. "You're kidding, right?"

"No, Robbie, your friend, that handsome young man Donavon, is indeed taking your sister to their prom. Your dad and I are both very pleased for Barbie. You should be too."

"When? When did this happen? Don never mentioned to me that he was asking you."

Robbie was still in a state of disbelief.

"Don asked me, Robbie. He doesn't need your permission, but to answer your question, he asked me yesterday after we finished giving our senior project in Cee Jay's class. By the way, we both got 'A's"

"mmm" Robbie suddenly felt sad. "I hope Donavon realizes what he's in for."

The women continued to make shopping plans. Robbie tried to block it out of mind as he ate his cereal, but the thought of Donavon asking his sister for a date without at least telling him bothered him. He knew that Barbie was right in saying that Don didn't need his permission, but he would have preferred if his friend had told him in advance.

As soon as he could, Robbie called Donavon. "What's this I hear about you taking my sister to the prom?"

"Man, news travels fast in Smallville," Don responded. "I was going to tell you about it, but it looks as though you already got the word."

"Yeah. Barbie's jumping all around the house this morning. How much did she have to pay you to take her?"

"Are you kidding? I was thinking about asking her for a long time, but I was too nervous to ask. It was awkward asking her. When she said 'yes,' I nearly fainted. I thought she may have already accepted someone else."

"You know you're crazy, Don…Barbie?…My sister?"

"Hey, Roberts. You should be happy for me. I get to take the prettiest, most intelligent, and nicest girl in Mountain Ridge High to my prom." Don paused. "And she just also happens to be my friend's sister. Look at it this way: I couldn't ask him to the prom, so I settled on his sister."

That was what Robbie needed to hear. It gave him the courage to endure the endless hours of dinner-time conversations related to the big event. It seemed that the prom was all his mom, sister, and even his dad could talk about all week. During the week details about the big night began to emerge. Donavon and Barbie would ride in Bob Walsh's car with Bob's date, a junior cheerleader by the name of Susan Meeger. Jamie insisted that Bob come into the house with Donavon when they came for Barbie. "I don't know this Bob Walsh; but if I smell any alcohol and detect any pot on him, so help me God, I'll chauffeur you around myself," Jamie dictated.

One night Robbie commented to his father: "Dad, can't you shut mom up about all this prom stuff? One would think she was going to the prom herself."

Jamie smiled and reached across the table for his wife's hand. "Maybe in a way, she is going to the prom. You see, Robbie, your mom never got to her own prom. She was too big carrying Barbie, and her husband, namely me, had to drop out of school. I was working the night of the prom. Barbie was born two days later. That's the reason neither of us got regular high school diplomas. Your mom got her GED first, and I got mine three years later, after you were born."

Melissa started crying. Barbie got up and wrapped her arms around her mother. "Mom, I love you. I'm going to dedicate a special dance just for you. I'll be thinking of both of you all night. I'll have a wonderful time, just for you." Going over to Jamie, she kissed him on the head. "Dad, I'm so proud of you. You're the best parents a kid can have."

The Saturday night event had arrived. Earlier Jamie had found his camera in the hall closet and made sure it was working properly. Taking a cue from Jamie, Robbie also got his own camera and placed it on the living room coffee table to be sure to get his own pictures. Melissa was in Barbie's room fussing with Barbie's hair and make-up. Jamie started the fireplace for, as he put it, 'the effect.' In order to ease the tension and awkwardness, Jamie and Robbie decided to play chess in the living room. It was determined that when the doorbell rang, Melissa would come down the stairs to answer the door. Barbie would make her grand entrance coming down the stairs a few minutes later.

At precisely 5:30, Donavon Rice and Robert Walsh arrived at the Roberts household, as per the plan. Melissa came down stairs to answer the door and greet the boys, call up to Barbie that they were there (as if she didn't know), and usher them into the living room to be greeted by father and son.

Jamie got up close and personal with Robert Walsh. He was glad to be assured that he would not be a chauffeur tonight. He warmly shook Robert's hand and then Donavon's. "You guys ready for the big night?" he asked. Turning to Melissa, he said, "These two really look terrific tonight. Don't they, honey? All shaved, polished, and dressed up in tuxedos. What do you think, Robbie?"

Up to this point Robbie was speechless. He always thought Donavon was handsome; but seeing him now, he thought he was gorgeous. Suddenly he wanted to grab him in his arms and kiss him. But, of course, he couldn't, so he just babbled something he later thought was ridiculous. "Yeah, you both look spiffy. Where did you leave your jeans and sneakers?" He regretted such a lame comment as soon as he said it, but both boys chuckled good naturedly.

Fortunately the awkward moment was broken with the sound of Barbie descending the stairs and entering the living room.

"Dah, dah," Barbie announced herself with a quick spin to show the boys her gown.

All four males in the room could only say "Wow!"

Jamie spoke first, "Honey, you look absolutely beautiful. Oh, if I weren't your father and eighteen years younger, I'd be fighting Donavon to take you to the prom myself."

"Well, sir, if I were eighteen years older, I'd be fighting you to take Mrs. Roberts to my prom. And to show you I'm serious, here, Mrs. Roberts. This bouquet is for you."

"Ah, my gosh, Donavon. How sweet of you!" She gave him a big hug and accepted the flowers.

"And these, my beautiful princess, are for you." Donavon handed Barbie a box containing the corsage of red roses that she had requested to highlight her off-white chiffon gown.

"Okay folks, this is where we start doing the Kodak moment stuff," Jamie said reaching for the camera on the coffee table. On cue, Robbie also picked up his digital camera "for back-up photos."

The three prom goers thought Jamie and Robbie were taking a million pictures, but in reality, they posed and gave fake smiles only eight times. Jamie and Robbie took pictures of Barbie alone showing off her full-length gown, satin shoes, and lace coverlet. Both boys posed in front of the fireplace. Bob was wearing an all-white tuxedo with tails, a white top hat, white shoes and a wide, white silk tie. Donavon's more conservative outfit consisted of black pants, black dressed shoes, a white jacket, white shirt, plaid cummerbund, and a plaid bow tie.

Pictures were taken of Donavon putting the corsage on Barbie's waist, of Barbie and Donavon gazing into one another's eyes, of Barbie between the two boys in front of the fireplace, and one of Melissa holding her bouquet with Barbie and Donavon on either side.

Donavon insisted that he use Mr. Roberts' camera to get a picture of Barbie and her two parents. When that photo was taken, Donavon said, "Let's get one more with Robbie this time." And so even Robbie had his picture taken on prom night, but he wished he was standing with Donavon. Robbie had shadowed his father in taking all the same poses that Jamie had taken, but Robbie managed to get a close-up facial and two full-body shots of Donavon alone.

As the excited teenagers were departing, there were more handshakes, hugs, and kisses. Even Robbie shook hands with Donavon and Bob and told them both to have a good time. Barbie was grateful that Jamie never brought up any mention of a curfew.

As soon as the parents closed the door after watching Bob Walsh's car pull out of their driveway, Robbie headed upstairs with his camera in his hands. "I have some reading to do for homework, so I'm going to my room for the night," he told his parents. But homework was not on his mind. He didn't want his parents to have the opportunity of seeing the close-up and full length pictures of Donavon alone that he took. He was anxious to see them himself, by himself, and then to erase them before the rest of the family saw them and started asking questions which he couldn't answer because even he didn't know why he took them.

All of Robbie's pictures were good. He thought that he might print out the one of Barbie with his mom and dad, but the solo shots of Donavon were great. He couldn't take his eyes off the facial close-up and kept running his fingers over the picture showing Don from head to toe.

God, he's gorgeous, Robbie found himself thinking. *I wish I could be going with him to the prom rather than Barbie, that conniving bitch. I wonder if she likes him as much as I do. Imagine having my arms around him. Having his body up against mine. I would just love to run my hands through his hair, to touch his face.*

He ran his fingers over the picture. *I wonder if he will kiss her tonight. What would that be like. Kissing Donavon.* The thought stirred his penis. *I wish I knew. Would I like kissing him as much as Barbie would? Would she get to see him without the jacket? Would she get to remove that plaid cummerbund and maybe reach in his pants to feel him?* Robbie felt his penis enlarging. He touched his own crotch. *This is crazy! Only a gay guy-or as mom says, a homosexual—would think like this. And I'm not gay. Hell, I never think of other guys the way I think of Don. I remember how he looked in his bathing suit at the Manor pool and spa. I wanted to touch him then. I've seen plenty of nude guys in the showers at school, and never gave a damn about any of them. Why do I have this feeling only for him? I got to get this guy out of my head. It's not right. What the fuck is wrong with me?*

Robbie tried reading his assignment, **The Old Man and the Sea**, but found concentrating on the novel difficult. His eyes roamed from the camera to the model air plane Donavon gave him and then back to the novel. Finally, he gave up the book and decided to look at the two solos of Don and delete them from his camera.

He tried reading again but the three days of Santiago's battle with the marlin just could not hold his interest. Robbie had his own battle to contend with. He decided to sleep it off, hoping that by tomorrow he would have a more realistic picture of Donavon. As he got under the covers, he wondered if the young couples were still dancing at the Country Club. He envisioned how wonderful Barbie must feel being in Donavon's arms. He envied his sister.

Thinking of Donavon's handsome face gave Robbie an erection once again. But this time he was in bed and wearing only the bottoms to his pajamas. He rolled over to grab the other pillow. He imagined the pillow was Donavon's body. His erection touched the sheets. Robbie touched it and swung the pillow up over him, imaging it to be Donavon. He wanted to touch Donavon's cock. Instead he pushed his own cock deep into the pillow. His body yearned to think of Don. He couldn't stop the want. He thought of nothing but holding Don in his arms. He ran his tongue around his own lips, trying to feel what it might be like to run his tongue against Don's lips. To kiss. To feel their tongues touch. He saw Don's face smiling at him in his imagination. Robbie ran his hands over the top of the pillow thinking he was running his hands through Don's full, thick hair. He would, if he could, put his hands on every part of Don's body. His lust could only be quenched by feeling his hand as if it were Don's. He felt an orgasm, an explosion of his own body releasing his juice into the pillow. He imagined Don smiling at him and kissing him as they both came.

Robbie knew it was just his imagination that went wild, but he liked it. He had lost himself in his lust. There could be no denying his desire. He now knew it was real. He felt his entire body relax. He rolled over and quickly fell into a peaceful sleep.

Chapter 17

THE NEXT MORNING ROBBIE awoke feeling refreshed but guilty. His guilt came upon realizing that he had ejaculated into the pillow next to him. He would have to wash it himself rather than have Barbie discovered it was soiled when she would do the family wash next Saturday. He checked to make sure that only the pillow case, not the pillow itself, was soiled, and was happy that the pillow was passable. Next, he felt guilty that he had masturbated while boldly thinking of Donavon.

Robbie thought, *With a guy, for god's sack! How gay is that? I've never really done that before. But come to think of it, I've never thought of a girl like that before either. Does that make me gay, or as mom would say, homosexual? God, just a few days ago I told her that I thought dad doing it with Cee Jay was 'disgusting,' and here I am jerking off thinking of Donavon. Donavon? Why him? I never thought of wanting sex with any other guy. How the hell am I going to face him again? How would he react if he knew I had the hots for him?...It's crazy! He's a football jock, for Christ's sake. And I'm a basketball center. Will he know by looking at me that I did it thinking of him? How can I hide it? ...Will I start acting silly like the other queer boys at school? How can I keep this a secret? ...I can't tell anyone, not even my best friend Roger Pucket...What the hell is wrong with me?*

He took a quick shower, dressed and went down stairs for breakfast. "Hi, mom, you're still home. I thought you would be at church."

"No, I'm skipping church today. I'm too tired and your father is still asleep. Both of us couldn't sleep well last night. I guess we were waiting up too late for Barbie to come home. I know your dad started snoring at two, and I must have dozed off sometime after that. But we both woke up when Barbie snuck in at four-thirty. Even though she was as quiet as a mouse, we woke up automatically. Your dad held me back from getting up to talk to her, and we both fell asleep again knowing that she was home safely. I'm anxious to hear how the prom went, but I'll have to wait until she gets up. Knowing her, that may not be until two o'clock; but I want to be here when she does."

Jamie and Robbie were finishing the chess game they began the night before and Melissa was reading the Sunday newspaper, when Barbie entered the living room in pajamas, her big bunny slippers, and something on her head. "Good morning, family," she said with a bright smile on her face.

"Why are you wearing that stupid looking crown on your head?" Robbie asked.

"Well, for starters, little brother, it's not a crown. It's a tiara. And I'm wearing it because I was named the queen of the prom last evening."

Jamie and Melissa both jumped up and grabbed her in their arms. Robbie remained seated and thought they were doing some kind of victory dance, like the pro teams do when they win a game. "Cee Jay told me yesterday afternoon that you probably would win, but I didn't want to say anything to ruin the surprise," Jamie said.

"Of course, Donavon was named king. I think he did a lot of politicking to get us elected. Remember, when he gave me the corsage, he called me his princess? If he had called me 'queen' he would have given it away. When Cee Jay and Dr. Jorgensen announced that Donavon and I were chosen king and queen, I was shocked. I nearly died when Donavon and I had to go on the dance floor all by ourselves. And, dad, Don must have known, because the number we danced to was one that Dr. S announced was chosen by Donavon as our favorite. Our favorite! Don and I never listened to music or danced before, but guess what it was?"

"Don't tell me. It was 'The First...'"

Barbie interrupted her father. "...Time Ever I Saw Your Face.' Your favorite! She emphasized the word 'your.'

"Actually, it's our song," Melissa said emphasizing the word 'our.' "Oh, how wonderful!"

"I should have been there to sing karaoke to it," Jamie said jokingly.

"You both were there," Barbie said. "I whispered that to Donavon as we danced."

"Is he a good dancer?"

"He's a wonderful dancer, mom. Even better than dad. He can dance to everything. Waltz, fox trot, polka, disco, ...anything. We even did a tango together. The guy's amazing!"

"So, sweetheart, you had a good time? Melissa asked.

"It was absolutely a magical night, mom" Barbie gushed.

"Well, let's all go into the kitchen and you can tell us all about it as I make you some breakfast."

In the kitchen, Barbie related the whole night to her parents who seemed to be hanging on every word and enjoying every bit of the replay. Robbie was uncharacteristically quiet. He listened but he had other things on his mind. Barbie related that when they arrived at the beautiful country club, the professional photographer took their pictures. The dinner was excellent. The band was very good; Johnny Shaw's brother sang very well. Cee Jay and Dr. Jorgensen made a few remarks and then opened the envelope to announce who won the election for king and queen. After she and Donavon danced to 'their' song, almost everyone got on the dance floor. Cee Jay and Miss Jorgensen also danced a slow one as well as several disco numbers. Even though the band was scheduled to stay and play until 10:30, some couples started to leave to go elsewhere as early as 9:30. Barbie, Donavon, Bob Walsh, and Susan Meeger had to leave at ten.

"Why did you have to leave then?" Jamie inquired.

"Because...and this was a total surprise also...Bob and Donavon had tickets for us at the Stone Pony in Asbury Park."

"Wow! That must have been terrific. I've always wanted to go there. Cee Jay and I went to the beach in Asbury Park many years ago, and he showed me the building."

"Just getting to be in the Stone Pony is exciting. Our tickets were for the midnight performance, which we all enjoyed. The place itself is like a museum of the great musical artists of our time. After the show, we went on the boardwalk, which is just across the street from the night club. We were practically the only people on the boardwalk. The four of us walked from one end to the other. Well, Don and I ran, arm in arm, part of the way. Bob and Susan decided to sit on what's like a pier at the Casino, while Donavon and I went back to sit on one of the boardwalk benches. I think we just sat there for over an hour just listening to the waves and taking and looking at the full moon and clouds. It was very nice."

"Sounds romantic," Jamie said.

"It was, dad. Very romantic!...If you're wondering if we made out, we did kiss. I like the way Donavon kisses. He's very romantic and very much a gentleman. But mostly we talked and got to really know one another better. I really like him, but neither one of us can get too serious. We both know that. He hopes to go away to Rutgers, and I want to go to Middlebury; but until September I hope we can go out together for a while. I enjoy his company. You know, dad, in many ways Donavon is like you."

Chapter 18

IN THE DAYS AFTER the prom, Robbie was despondent. He still could not explain his feelings for Donavon. Since he had not heard from the senior boy, he felt that Don no longer cared for him. He thought that now Donavon was more interested in Barbie than himself. Indeed, Donavon had actually called the Roberts house twice, but not to talk to Robbie. Donavon had made a date with Barbie to go to a movie. In doing so, however, he established the fact that it would be 'Dutch treat' and Bob Walsh and Susan Meeker would 'double date' with them. Bob would be the driver to the theater at the mall in Budd Lake. Afterward they could hang out in the food court and arcade and go to the record store. Barbie readily agreed, but stated that she also wanted to browse in Barnes & Noble. She said that she was looking for *Jane Eyre*, a novel that Dr. Seton had recommended she read for college.

Of course, the next day Robbie had to suffer through Barbie's talking incessantly all about the movie date and her holding hands all day with Donavon and how much fun they had at the mall. Robbie could have strangled her when she told her mother that she was 'falling for him.'

One afternoon Robbie was so distraught that he smashed the model airplane that Donavon had made with him and then gave to him to keep. Robbie remembered how much he enjoyed making that plane because of Donavon. He also remembered how Don cut his finger and he cut his own so they could be blood brothers. "*Yeah, blood brothers my ass. More like brothers-in-law,*" he thought. He threw the broken pieces of the model in the waste basket. *If only I can get him out of my mind as easily as I broke his fucking model.*

He asked Roger Pucket to go bicycling with him, but it rained on the planned day. He invited Roger to come over to his house; but when Roger came, they only shot hoops in the driveway for a while. Robbie really was not enjoying it. Roger eventually said that he had promised his mother that he would watch his little sister while she went shopping. Robbie knew Roger made up this story just to leave, but he was glad, because he wasn't interested in his old friend any way. He was yearning to do things with Donavon.

One day, Robbie noticed that Donavon and Bob were no longer surrounded by their jock friends in the lunch room. Now, sitting at the table across from the football players were Barbie and Susan Meeker. Robbie felt he had been stabbed in the back and suddenly felt nauseous. His reaction must have been obvious because Roger Pucket's girlfriend Judy Ferrero asked him if something was wrong. "Man, you look like you just saw a ghost," she said.

"No, not a ghost," Robbie snapped back. "More like the devil."

"Does it have anything to do with your sister having lunch over there with Donavon Rice? I hear they're an item now."

"Yeah, something like that," Robbie said.

"You wanna talk about it?"

"No, I...I can't right now." Robbie wondered if he could talk to anyone about how he really felt about Donavon. He knew his obsession had to stop, though. It was driving him crazy, and he knew he needed help. The question was: Help from whom?

During the next week, the halls at school were buzzing with news of college acceptance letters, which were being received. Through the grapevine, Robbie learned that Bob Walsh was accepted at U. Conn. And would get financial assistance for playing basketball. Donavon got into Rutgers on an academic scholarship and financial assistance through the Rotary and Boy Scouts. He would also get financial help if he played football for the Scarlet Knights. The Roberts house was jumping over Barbie's acceptance with academic scholarships to both Carnegie Mellon in Pittsburg and Middlebury in Vermont. She only had a short time to choose which one to go to. She was getting advice from everyone: mom, dad, Cee Jay, and her guidance counselor. It was a tough decision. She felt that her entire future depended on what college she should go to. All the pros and cons were considered and reconsidered.

Robbie felt cut-off from his family, especially his father who seemed to be more interested in things related to Barbie. He couldn't wait for September when both Barbie and Donavon would be out of his life. He was surprised, however, that in all of this talk about going away to college, Barbie never mentioned how she felt about the fact that she and Donavon would be separating. But September was still several months away. *"If I liked Don as much as she does, I wouldn't want to go to a college so far away from his. If he goes to Rutgers, I would too," Robbie reasoned. "Maybe I'll go to Rutgers myself."*

Robbie went into the library during a study hall period to find a book on jet propulsion. There he saw Cee Jay sitting at a table by himself. The teacher seemed lost in a book he was reading.

Impulsively, Robbie went over to him. "Hi, Dr. S," he said sitting opposite.

Cee Jay seemed surprised. "Oh, hello, Robbie. How are you?"

"Well, to tell you the truth, Dr. S, I do have a real problem, and I was wondering if you might help me with it."

"I'll certainly try to. What's troubling you?"

Suddenly Robbie realized that he may have made a mistake by even mentioning his problem to his father's lover. However, Cee jay was gay, fairly easy to talk to, and an intelligent adult. After a pause, Robbie responded, "Well, it's something I can't talk about right here at school." He looked around the library, "and I absolutely don't want you to mention a word about it to my dad. He can't know that I even mentioned any problem to you."

"Okay, my lips are sealed, at least until I learn more about the problem. If I can help without your father knowing about it, I'll try to help as much as possible. Is that okay with you?"

"I...I guess so."

"Since you don't want anyone to know about it, would you feel comfortable meeting me at the gazebo in the park tomorrow afternoon. Would four o'clock work for you?"

"Yes, that would be great, Dr. S. See you then." Getting up he shook Cee Jay's hand. "Thanks a lot."

The next day, Robbie rode his bicycle to the park. He gave himself enough time to be sure to be there before the planned four o'clock meeting. He didn't want to give Cee Jay any idea that he was chickening out even though he had thought of doing so. He was nervous about making his confession, but he had given it much thought since he first approached Cee Jay yesterday, and still felt Cee Jay was the best person to whom he could discuss his relationship with Donavon. Robbie needed to see this through, no matter what happened.

Sure enough, Cee Jay was right on time, but what was strange was that the teacher had bicycled to the park. Robbie just imagined that he would drive over in his old Chevy. Instead, here he was in sweat pants, a tee shirt, sneakers, and a bike helmet. This was something he might expect from his father, not Cee Jay.

Cee Jay got right down to business. "So, young man, what's your big secret problem that you can't discuss with your dad, but can with your father's gay lover?"

Wow, Cee Jay came right to the point. That put Robbie at ease immediately. There would be no pretense here.

"Okay, well, here goes. You see, Dr. S, there's this boy at school, and…"

Cee Jay interrupted him. "By 'this boy at school,' am I correct in assuming you mean Donavon Rice?"

"Yes, how did you know I meant Donavon?"

"Just a guess, but go on. What do you want to tell me about Donavon?"

"Well, since I met him in the Poconos that time we went skiing, we became friends." He paused not quite sure what to say next.

"Yes, Robbie, I know you became close." He smiled. "I guess we all became friendlier with Donavon. Should I say, particularly your sister Barbie?"

"Yeah, her too, but even more, me," Robbie said at length.

"Are you jealous of Barbie?"

"Yes."

"mmm. Tell me about that, Robbie. What accounts for your jealousy?"

"That's just it. I don't know why. I love my sister, but maybe she is able to like Donavon in a way that I can't."

"Do you love Donavon, Robbie?" He emphasized the word 'you.'

"I don't know. Maybe."

Cee Jay paused. "A moment ago, you said that Barbie was able to like Donavon in a way that you couldn't. Did you mean that she could openly express her affection for Donavon and you couldn't?"

"Yes, exactly."

"How would you want to express your liking—or love—for Donavon?"

"I'm not gay!" Robbie blurted out defensively.

Again, Cee Jay thought carefully about what to say next. "Robbie, I did not intend to suggest that I thought you were gay. Let me ask you, though. Do you think your affection for Donavon may be an indication to you that you might be gay?"

"Yeah, that's it. I've never thought of any guy in the way I think about Donavon. But I've never given much thought to girls either. Donavon's the first person—male or female—that I ever thought of, you know, in a physical way."

"By 'physical way,' do you mean sexually?"

Robbie nodded his head and paused before finally letting it out. "Yes."

"Have you and Donavon ever done anything together that you might consider sexual?"

"Yes and no. Nothing together, I mean."

"But you have thought of him that way while by yourself?"

"Yes."

"Robbie, do you think Donavon is gay?" Cee Jay asked.

"Donavon?...Gay?...Hell no! He's super macho. He's a football player. He's dating my sister, for Christ's sake. According to her, they're always holding hands and kissing."

"Do you think they have gone beyond that? Do you think they have actually had sex?"

145

"Not yet at any rate, but …" Robbie paused.

"But?…But what?…Why did you stop?"

"Donavon did tell me once that he dates a lot of girls, but never gets serious with any of them. He told me that he wants to graduate from college before he thinks of girls seriously."

"There you go, Robbie. I think you may have just answered your own concerns."

"I don't understand."

"Robbie, let's look at it like this: If you could have a physical relation—sex—with Donavon, would you wait until you were out of college?"

"Hell, no! I guess I wouldn't even wait to finished junior year in high school."

"You know, Robbie, it is possible that Donavon is even more conflicted than you are about his own sexuality. Right now, neither of us can truly know what Donavon thinks. I think I can understand Donavon though, because I too fought that private battle. Donavon is eighteen. I didn't accept my own sexual leanings until I was working on my doctorate. I was twenty-three. That was just about the same time I met your father.

"I knew even then, that your dad liked me, but like the naïve jerk I was back then, I never gave him the opportunity. Now, I realize how much I missed by not giving him the love he was offering back then. I thank God, that we found one another after so many years, but I do regret what I've missed. I hope that neither you nor Donavon ever have to have such regrets. You both should be true to your own natures. Donavon may turn out to be one hundred percent straight; but frankly, between you and me, I doubt it. Some men become good family men but cheat with other men or women indiscriminately. That's very dangerous. A few men are bi-sexual. I guess your dad and I are among the very rare ones. He has a wonderful wife and family, and I have him and we all have one another. There are no secrets.

"The guys I feel sorry for are the ones who deny their feelings all their lives. They get into miserable marriages and make life miserable for themselves and their families. In one of his plays, Shakespeare wrote the greatest advice a man can give: 'Unto thine own self be true.' So, let that be my advice to you too, Robbie. Follow your own instincts."

"Funny, my mom said practically the same thing to me just a few weeks ago."

"Your mother, Robbie, is very intuitive and one of the best people I know in the world."

"So, what I hear you saying is that I am gay."

"Not at all, Robbie. What I am saying is that it doesn't matter what you are as long as you are happy to be the person that God created you to be."

"So, how do I stop thinking about Donavon?"

"You probably never will forget Donavon. Most people never forget their first love, male or female. Even when you're old and gray, Robbie, you'll think back to today and wonder the great 'What if' questions of life. You know: 'What if I told Donavon I loved him, what if he had told you, what if he didn't move away to go to college?' You do know, don't you, that he's going to Rutgers in a few months? You may never see him again. Everyone loses friends—dear friends sometimes—as we go through life. It's sad, difficult, but often inevitable. You'll meet new friends, have new experiences, and in time as you do, the hurt you now feel will gradually diminish; but you will probably always fondly remember Donavon." Cee Jay stopped for a moment.

"Robbie, how old are you?

"Seventeen. I'll be eighteen in July."

"Does Donavon know that?"

"I don't know. But what difference does it make?"

"Well, Donavon may be trying to protect you...and himself. He simply may be waiting until you become legal." Cee Jay paused and smiled. "This is New Jersey, you know; and our legislators still haven't accepted the fact that some teenagers can—and do have consenting sex before their eighteenth birthday."

"Really? You got to be kidding me?"

"Really," Cee Jay said. "Regardless of what you hear in the halls and locker rooms at school, if an eighteen year-old has sex with someone under eighteen, it's legally considered rape."

"That's crazy!"

"Not necessarily, Robbie. "In a couple of months, you may understand the wisdom of it; but for now, you must try. In the meantime, however, Donavon may be wrestling with another problem."

"What's that?"

"Donavon is a Roman Catholic. His church still holds that sex between people of the same sex, is a sin. If Donavon believes that, he may be having a big struggle."

"Wow! I didn't realize that."

"Yes, that can be a tough issue for many Catholics."

There was silence between the two.

"'Amor vincit omnia.'"

"Huh? What's that?"

"It's Latin, Robbie, for 'Love conquers all,' a famous expression."

"Oh. It seems Donavon has a lot to conquer."

"And, so do you, Robbie. A lot of kids in their early teens, who are awakening to their sexuality develop crushes or love for an older friend. It's a little like hero worship. Teachers, priests, and others who work with young people are often aware of this and must be on guard, because sometimes those feelings are very dangerous. Your feelings at the present time for Donavon don't make you gay. You told me that you never thought about sex with any specific boy or girl before. I take it you don't look at pictures in **Blue Boy** or **Play Boy**. That's usually an indicator of preference. If you actually had sex with a boy and liked it and wanted more, that too would be an indicator of your preference."

There was a long pause before Cee Jay spoke again.

"Robbie, has Donavon ever said anything to you that made you think he was trying to suggest that the two of you do something that you thought might be sexual?"

"No."

"Has he ever touched you in a way that made you feel embarrassed or uncomfortable or that made you think that he wanted to touch you in a sexual way?"

"No, not really."

"What do mean 'not really'?"

"Well, he did put his arm around my shoulder, and once or twice he hugged me. You know, like teammates do after they score in a game. Jocks do it all the time." Robbie paused. "Dr. S, why is it that jocks talk dirty about girls in the locker room and then hug one another on the field or court? No one thinks that's gay."

"Welcome to the adult world, Robbie, where peer pressure and society dictate what's considered appropriate and not appropriate. When Donavon put his arms around you and hugged you, did you like it?"

"To tell you the truth, the first time he did it, I was surprised. Later, I liked it and wanted him to be close like that and do it again. But he almost never did."

"I see. Peer pressure may be another struggle for Donavon. Among teens in high school, peer pressure is very strong. Robbie, did you ever talk to Donavon about how you felt about him?"

"No. I couldn't do that."

"Why not?"

Robbie thought about his answer to this question. "I...I... don't think I could explain myself correctly to him. And, if he didn't feel the same way, he might think I was crazy or something and never want to talk to me again."

"You think that would end your relationship with him?"

"Yeah, probably."

"But you just told me that—and I'm quoting you here—'if he didn't feel the same way about me.' So, in other words, you want him to like you the same way. Robbie, isn't it possible that he does like you that way, but he also feels unsure of your reaction?"

Robbie stretched out his one-word answer as a question: "Y…e…s…?"

"I think you should be patient, bear it a while longer, see what happens; but give him the opportunity to make the first move. At any rate, don't lose him as a friend. You both may feel a lot different about your friendship when he goes away to college.

"One thing you should not do is shut Donavon out of your life now. Enjoy your friendship with him every day while you still have time together. Build pleasant memories you both may savor someday. Remember that other Latin expression 'carpe diem.' It means 'seize the day.' We must make the most of the time God gives us on this planet. Be a good friend to Donavon, and who knows what path that friendship may ultimately take."

Robbie was deep in thought, but momentarily began to cry. "Thank you for talking to me and giving me your insights and advice. It's help me understand not only things about myself and Don, but others as well." He took out a handkerchief to wipe his eyes.

He got up at the same time the mentor did. Robbie went to him and put both arms around him in a tight hug. "I love you, Cee Jay," he said.

"I love you too, Robbie; but remember, at school it's 'Dr. S.' Okay?"

Chapter 19

TWO DAYS AFTER ROBBIE had the talk with Cee Jay, Donavon called the Roberts household; but when Melissa answered the phone, she was somewhat surprised to learn that he wanted to speak to Robbie. Melissa thought at first that Donavon was calling to plan a date or something with Barbie.

Robbie took the telephone from his mother. "Hello."

"Hi, Robert, Donavon here. How are you, buddy?"

"Ah, okay. What's up?"

"I've been pretty busy working at Mickey D's and studying for finals. Gosh, it's hard to believe, I'll be graduating in a couple of weeks. The little time I get free lately seems to be taken up by the Roberts family. I guess you heard all about the prom from Barbie. It really was awesome, and I'm glad that I finally got up enough nerve to ask her. You have a great sister, Robert."

"You can call, me Robbie," he interrupted.

"Okay. Robert is too formal anyway. As I was saying, Barbie is a lot of fun to be with. We went to the mall last week with Walsh and Susan. But now I want to spend some time with the other Roberts, namely you. I have a great idea, if you are up to it on Sunday."

"What do you have in mind?"

"Exercise, man. Exercise! Get those leg muscles going again. I bet you haven't been doing too much since basketball season ended."

"You got that right. So what kind of exercise are you planning?"

"An all-day bike ride to Sunrise Mountain."

"Sunrise Mountain? Where is it?"

"It's part of Stokes State Forest. It's one of my favorite places in Sussex County. I'm surprised you have never been there. You'll love it. It's at a high elevation, so part of the trip we'll be pedaling uphill quite a bit, but coming down you can relax and cruise."

Robbie thought for a moment. *If you love it, I'll love being there with you.*

"We can take our time getting there and back, because I'm off all day Sunday."

"Who all is going?" Robbie asked.

"Just you and me, buddy. It's been awhile, so this will be our adventure."

"Okay, then, I'll go. We did have fun riding to the park that time."

After discussing some details such as where to meet, what time, what to wear and what to bring such as a backpack with stuff to eat and drink, their trip was set.

"Oh, and be sure to bring your camera. There are some beautiful picture spots along the way and from the look out when we get there," Donavon added. "I'll bring my field glasses."

Robbie was thrilled that Donavon had called him. He was also glad that Barbie, Bob Walsh and his girlfriend would not be going. This would be a day with just the two of them. It didn't matter to him where they were going. Don wanted him to go with him, and he would have gone anywhere if it meant being with Don.

The boys met as planned at the gazebo in the park at ten o'clock Sunday morning. Robbie almost melted when he saw Donavon approach. Don was wearing the tightest, faded jeans imaginable. He also had a long-sleeve, bright red jersey with "Rutgers" written with big white letters; "The State University" was written in smaller letters beneath it. The sunlight was reflecting off his wrap-around sun glasses.

The weather was perfect for cycling. The sky was a beautiful blue with just a few puffy clouds to accentuate the clean, clear air of northern New Jersey. The temperature was just right for this 'adventure' at the end of May. On their way to the State Park, the teenagers past several large dairy farms and a few new housing developments that were taking the place of former farms. The gentle rolling hills of Sussex Country still gave the area a bucolic atmosphere. Here and there a barn and silo pierced the landscape. The air seemed permeated with the smells of freshly cut bundles of hay.

Robbie took several pictures of a farmer shepherding a herd of cows across the road.

"Only in Sussex County will you still see something like this," Donavon said. "That's what I love about this place."

Robbie had Donavon pose for several pictures. Today he was not embarrassed to take full body and close-up facial pictures. Donavon asked Robbie to pose for a picture in front of an old, deserted stone house that stood above a dirt road a short distance from the road.

For most of the trip the boys rode side by side when traffic was light. When cars wanted to pass, Robbie slowed down for Don to take the lead. On more than one of those occasions Robbie was able to get a sneak photo of Donavon from the back, including a close-up of his ass.

The road leading up the mountain was difficult to pedal and required greater effort.

"Is this what you meant by exercise?" Robbie yelled ahead to Donavon.

"Yeah, it's good for your leg muscles as well as your lungs. Ah, smell those pine trees! This is God's country, Robbie," Don yelled back. "Want to stop and rest?"

"No, let's keep going. We can rest when we get to the over-look."

The view from the observation point truly was spectacular. Below them were gentle hills filled with greenery and a few small lakes and farm watering ponds.

A few cars were parked in an area along the edge. "People come up here very early to see the sun rise on the horizon. That's New York way over there," Donavon explained. "On Easter Sunday, sun rise services are held here, but I've never been here for Easter. Would like to, though. Maybe someday you and I can come up here to actually see the sun rise. Some of the people from those cars may have been here since early morning. It's a great place to come for a picnic. There are barbeque pits and some tables in the pavilion."

"Wow!" Robbie commented. "Imagine being up here in a thunderstorm. It must be better than watching fireworks."

"In the fall, with the leaves changing colors, it's beautiful. I've never been here in the winter with snow on the hills and trees, but I bet it's just as spectacular."

"Now, I know why you said it is one of your favorite places," Robbie said.

"I'm glad that you are with me. Now I can share it with you. It's now our special place." Don put emphasis on the words "our special."

Robbie remembered the advice Cee Jay had given him. *Carpe diem.* He was indeed seizing the opportunity of the day. He was with Donavon, and he was having a time which he knew he would long remember.

"What's that big lake over there, Don?"

"That's Culvers Lake. I'll be a life guard and swim instructor at the Boy Scout day camp there as soon as school's over. I'll work there through Labor Day. The camp is on a cove to our left." Donavon tried spotting the camp with his binoculars.

"Here, you can make out a few of the camp cabins." He handed the field glasses to Robbie who had difficulty focusing on the area Don described. Donavon went behind Robbie and adjusted the lens for Robbie then moved the glasses in the direction of the camp. "Do you see it now?" Robbie did see what looked like cabins around a cove that had a raft in the middle, but he was concentrating more on Don's breath on his neck and the warmth of his body against his own.

"You will have to come to the camp someday. The camp closes at five, and is closed on Sundays. We can have the whole place to ourselves."

"What kind of a camp is it?"

"It's for scouts between six and twelve or thirteen. We don't have any high school kids. The boys are dropped off about eight in the morning and stay until we close at five. It's strictly a day camp; we don't do any overnight camping at the Culver Lake site. They learn to swim, and we have all kinds of water sport activities like rowing, boarding, races, polo, etc. We also have a hall where they can play all sorts of chess and other board games. When it's raining, we usually show movies. We serve a good lunch for the boys. The chef is really good. This will be my third summer working there but my first as head life guard and swim instructor. I really enjoy it."

"How much does it cost?"

"I'm not really sure. If I remember correctly, last year the parents had to pay fifty dollars for the ten-week program. But, of course, we get a lot of donations from local businesses. I know the Rotary contributes a lot to pay the salaries of counselors and others who work around the place.

The boys sat opposite one another to have the lunches they brought in their back packs. When it was time to leave the

Sunrise Mountain lookout, both boys agreed that it was worth the effort, good exercise, and agreed to do it again some time.

The trip home was a lot easier, as Donavon had said it would be. Robbie was glad that he was a good friend of Don. Cee Jay was right in telling him to be patient, and just enjoy the time they were having now, and not to expect more than either one of them could give at present. In the meantime, he had those pictures in his camera to look forward to at home.

Chapter 20

EVERYONE KNOWS THAT GRADUATION is inevitable. It happens. Everyone waits for it, hopes for it, and can't wait for it to be over. When it does occur, however, no one can believe that it is actually happening. Everything suddenly seems to be moving too quickly. First was the prom, then the whole college acceptance frenzy. One day, yearbooks are distributed. You go around signing them and telling everyone how much you love them and will never forget them. The next day you are practicing a new way to walk to a new tune called "Pomp and Circumstances" or as Barbie Roberts called it: "The Children's Marching Song."

Barbie remembered the road trips she took with her mother and father to visit colleges in Vermont one weekend and in Pennsylvania the next. She thought of that evening at the 'Open House—Back to School', when her dad reunited with his old pal, who just happened to be her favorite teacher. She always suspected something between her dad and the teacher, but she vividly remembered that afternoon a few days before New Year's when her mom told her the full story. Barbie reminisced about Donavon Rice and working on the project and getting to know and like him. She would always remember that wonderful prom at which she and Don were named king and queen. *In the far future,* she thought, *I hope to meet a man to marry who is as handsome, intelligent, charming, and fun to be with as Donavon Rice.*

For all 123 graduates of Mountain Ridge High School, it was a time to reflect. They thought of good times, bad times, funny times. Some of them remembered their first real sexual experiences. There were some loses and some wins.

Donavon Rice, remembered winning football games and getting awards in Scouting. Donavon also had memories of meeting Robbie at the Pocono Manor with his father Jamie and his English teacher. He remembered how much fun it was to watch Robbie play basketball and to make a model air plane with him. He thought of when they flew the radio-controlled model in the park. He especially liked going to Sunrise Mountain with Robbie. His life now seemed to have revolved around the Roberts family a great deal, and through them, got to know his teacher on a more personal level. Don really enjoyed working with Barbie on the English project and going to the prom with her. Don especially liked the fact that she never pushed him into a serious dating situation like so many of the other girls did. He fondly remembered the day after school that he gave Robbie one of his wallet-sized yearbook pictures, and how Robbie was so happy to get it, he starting crying. Donavon had also grown to very much like and admire Mr. Roberts, a man who was more to him as a father than his own step-dad. Donavon wished that he could always remain close to Dr. Seton and the entire Roberts family.

A member of the United States Senate, who actually attended Mountain Ridge High School himself, was the main speaker at the commencement in mid-June. He spoke on following your dreams and believing in yourself and loving God and country. It was a great speech, but a few hours later none of the graduates could remember a word he said except for his last sentence, which was "Now go out there and capture your dreams!" which he practically shouted into the microphone.

Jamie's and his crew had finished Cee Jay's 'man cave' just in time for its 'christening' on graduation day. The guests of honor, of course, were Barbie and Donavon. In addition to Cee Jay, who was hosting the party were Donavon's mother, Mrs. Betty Fitzgerald, who went by her married name, rather than Rice, which was her first husband's name. Her husband, Don's step-father, could not be there. She said that her husband, who was a truck driver, had to drive a semi down to Florida. Jamie, Melissa, and Robbie, of course, were there. Marylyn Jorgensen, the French teacher and foreign language department chair who was class adviser and chaperone at the prom, was also invited. Bob Walsh and his girlfriend Susan rounded out the guest list.

Donavon was anxious to see the final result of his ideas and Jamie's construction. There were quite a few changes made. Most notable of the changes was that rather than a half-bath, Jamie built a full bathroom, including a country tub. Also added to the final project was a small entry foyer with a door on ground level which covered the original cellar opening outside. The galley kitchen was a bit larger than Donavon's original drawing and the 'theater room' was not tiered, and rather than school auditorium seats, there were only two, big leather recliner chairs.

A small closet was built into one wall which extended into the laundry room. Cee Jay and Jamie explained to Don and the other guests that were listening that they built the extension over where the stairs leading outside were because it might be possible for Cee Jay to rent out the basement, thus giving the renter a separate, private entrance. Jamie felt that this added feature would greatly increase the value of the house. The 'theater room' because it now contained a closet could be considered a bedroom, if so desired. That was also the rationale for making the kitchen area larger as well. Everyone, including Donavon liked the 'man cave'. Dr. Jorgensen said that she thought it would make a great 'bachelor pad,' if Cee Jay decided to rent it out.

Cee Jay had an open bar of liquor drinks for the adults and a variety of sodas for the teens, although everyone was treated to a champagne toast which Cee Jay gave to the graduates and their parents. He had prepared trays of salads, cold cuts, cakes, etc. which were served buffet style. After eating, the teens played a variety of games. Robbie and Bob Walsh played chess, while Donavon, Susan and Barbie played Scrabble.

At four o'clock Bob announced that it was time to head out. Several members of their class had invited them to their house parties, so it was time for them to hit the road and 'make the rounds.'

"I'll make sure that Barbie's home safe, sound, and sober by ten o'clock, Mr. Roberts," Donavon said as they were leaving.

"You better," Jamie said authoritatively.

After the graduates and Susan left, the adults and Robbie stayed on to party some more. Jokes were told, and Jamie entertained with his karaoke routines. Melissa joined in for two songs. The adults reminisced about when the graduates were in first grade, and then did some disco dancing. Robbie disappeared into the 'theater room' to watch the Yankees-Mets game on Cee Jay's large screen projector TV.

The 'man cave' christening and graduation party ended at nine, when Jamie said he wanted to be home 'before his little girl.' Mrs. Fitzgerald and Marylyn Jorgensen left together saying they both had a good time. Betty said she was proud of her son and thanked Cee Jae and Jamie for taking her son 'under their wings.' "He speaks so highly of both of you," she said. Melissa, who suspected her husband may have had too many martinis, told Jamie that she was driving.

Chapter 21

THE BIG NEWS THAT Barbie had for her family when Bob Walsh dropped her off at 9:15 was that Donavon's grandparents had surprised him with a car. Of course, it was a used car, and a Volkswagen Beetle at that; but Donavon was really amazed and grateful. Because Don lived closest to the last party they attended, he was taken to his own home first, and as Bob pulled into Don's driveway, they saw Don's mother and grandparents standing around the yellow beetle. Barbie relayed to her family the whole scene as she remembered it.

"What's going on?" Don had said getting out of Bob's car.

"What's going on, Donavon, is that your grandmother and I want to give you these." Mr. Rice put a set of keys in Don's hand. "This car is both your graduation and nineteenth birthday gift. We know that if your father were still alive, this gift would have been from him. We know that you will need a car to go to college. Your mother has agreed to pay the extra premium to put you on her insurance, but you will have to pay for gas and maintenance on your own."

Barbie relayed to her family how Don was so thrilled that he actually started to cry. She told her family how she and Bob jumped out of Walsh's car to congratulate Don and examine his yellow beetle. Don insisted that his first passengers would be Bob and Barbie because Bob had actually been teaching him how to drive with a shift gear on his own car. They only drove around a few blocks before getting back to his house, but Don was very proud that now he had a car.

The next day Donavon called Robbie to tell him about the car.

"Yeah, Barbie told us all about it when she got home last night. That's great news, Don." He paused. "But I hope you and I can still go bike riding together once in a while."

"Of course, we will, Roberts!" Don paused. "Say, I start working on Monday at the Day Camp. How about I pick you up on Sunday, show you my yellow beetle, and we take a drive up to Sunrise Mountain. This time we can drive and we don't have to pedal our butts off to get to our special place."

Robbie instantly remembered Donavon referring to Sunrise Mountain as their 'special place.'

"That sounds excellent, Don. Let's go!"

"Super! I'll pick you up at twelve next Sunday."

"So, now that school's out, what will you be doing all summer?" Donavon inquired.

"I don't know yet, but I'm sure mom and dad will keep me busy with chores at home and at dad's office. When dad comes home from work, he and I usually play one-on-one; and Pucket and I will probably hang out an' go to the park a lot on our bikes. Nothing special, though. Maybe you and me can make another model air plane."

"Hey that sounds great. Maybe the four of us can fly your radio-controlled model in the park again."

"Yeah, that's an idea. Well, I'll see you on Sunday. Bye."

The summer had begun. Robbie was happy that he would be spending some quality time with Donavon and Roger. Barbie had started her job as a summer fill-in receptionist at the Newton Hospital and would also be busy getting ready for her new life as a college student and living away from home for the first time. The summer months were the busiest in the construction and contracting business, so Jamie and Melissa would be working longer and harder. Robbie was looking forward to his eighteenth birthday party on July 10. Jamie told his family that Cee Jay had made plans to go to the Costa del Sol of Spain for three weeks but would not miss Robbie's birthday party. Cee Jay was going with another teacher friend from Frankford High School. Jamie said that he wished he could go with him, but maybe next winter the two of them could get away together for a vacation around Christmas.

Everyone in the Roberts house heard the "beep, beep, beep" of the Beetle on Sunday. Robbie was ready with his camera in his back pack. He grabbed a Gatorade and a trail mix bar before heading out. "We'll be having dinner at five, so be sure you are home by then," Melissa called to Robbie from the kitchen. "Ask Donavon to join us for dinner, if he wants." Robbie was closing the front door, when she said, "Have fun, honey."

Donavon was standing beside the open door of the Volkswagen. He gave Robbie a big hand shake, the kind you may give to someone you hadn't seen in years. Robbie liked that. He was thrilled to be riding in Don's car. He thought it was just like its owner: bright, simple but complex, efficient, not too showy, fashionable, and—above all—fun. The radio was tuned to a country/ western station that both boys decided they liked while they were working on Donavon's air plane. Donavon told him that the only other station he could pick up was a "Jesus saves" station that only played gospel music mixed with a lot of preaching and asking for donations to "keep the word of God alive in Sussex County."

Robbie laughed. "Yeah, and the coffers of the Reverend Billy Sanders full."

Don spread out a blanket on a grassy area near the picnic tables at the Sunrise lookout. Robbie tossed his backpack on the blanket and stretched out next to Donavon. The two young men lay there in silence. They both were enjoying the fantastic view, the cool breezes and the chirping of the birds. Above them the sky was a beautiful blue.

After a while, Don said, "A penny for your thoughts, Roberts."

"I was just thinking about your calling this 'our special place.' I'm glad it is, and I'm glad we're such friends…Special friends, I mean."

Donavon rolled over to his side and used his elbow to raise himself in order to look down at Robbie. The two boys just stared into one another's eyes. In a low voice, almost whispering, Donavon said, "You are, you know. My special friend. I hope you always will be." He rolled back to face the sky.

"I promise," Robbie said.

Robbie wanted to grab Don's hand, to hold it tight; but he was too afraid. He wanted to roll over and kiss him, but he was afraid. He wanted to put his arms around him and hold him, but he was afraid. Instead, both boys remained silent, not able to exhibit or verbalize the feelings they both were experiencing.

"You know, I'll be eighteen on July tenth, Don. It's a Thursday, so I hope you will be able to come to my birthday party. It will start about six, so you can come after working at the camp."

"You betcha I'll be there. I wouldn't miss my special friends' eighteenth big one for anything. Who all will be there?"

"You mean besides you and me?"

"Well, yeah. Not that it really matters though. We can have a party with just the two of us."

"Okay, for starters, there will be mom, dad, Barbie, and, of course, Cee Jay. By the way Cee Jay is going to Spain right after my birthday."

"Cool! I'd love to go to Spain too. Who's he going with? Dr. Jorgensen?"

"No. Dad said he's going to the Costa del Sol with another male teacher from Frankford."

"Good for him. Maybe someday you and I can go on a trip like that, Roberts."

"I'll remember that when I blow out the candles on my cake, Rice."

"Okay, so who else are you inviting?"

"Let's see. Roger Pucket, of course, and Judy Ferrero; Bob Walsh and Susan and probably some of the basketball players. That's about it, I guess. Mom and Cee jay will prepare some food, dad will make sure our pool is ready for use. He will also provide music and singing, and Barbie is always in charge of decorations. I'll have to remind everyone to bring bathing suits."

"Are You excited about having your eighteenth birthday?" Don hesitated for a moment. "I'm sure the party will be great."

"Of course, birthdays are always fun. You know, cards, gifts, cake, all that blowing out of candles stuff. But this year I guess it pretty much means the end of that kiddy stuff. I'll be legally an adult and have to pay adult prices at the movies. And, hell, I'm a senior now in high school. I can't believe it." He paused. "Hey, when is your birthday?"

"I'll be nineteen on August twenty-one. I'm just a year and a month or so older than you, buddy."

"Really? Barbie's is on August twentieth. This year, we can celebrate with a big bash for both of you. It can also be a going away party for both of you. I have to talk to my mom and dad about it, but I'm sure Barbie would love the idea. Dad's always up for a party."

"That sounds very good. I like your thinking, Roberts. Now, let's take a little hike. There's a nice trial along the rim."

Robbie instantly stood and took his camera out of the backpack before strapping it onto himself. Don led the way to the trail. They spent a few hours walking and talking along the path. They stopped to take pictures of one another as well as the flora and fauna. Robbie actually got a few relatively close pictures of a deer and doe.

Along the trail, the path became divided. Donavon used this to impress Robbie with his memorization of poetry. "Two roads diverged in a yellow wood/ And I, I took the one less traveled by."

"Very good, Mr. Frost," Robbie said while clapping. "Now, as Dr. Cee Jay Seton would analyze it, are you going to stay at home and go to Sussex Community and Montclair State or go to Rutgers?"

"Oh, definitely Rutgers."

"Okay, so what will you study: engineering and architecture or law and business?"

"Ah, those two paths divide farther down the trail, and we have many miles to go before we reach them."

Both boys smiled at one another. "Thou art indeed a scholar, Mr. Rice. Dr. Seton would be proud of his protégé."

"We better start heading back to the beetle, if I'm to get you home in time for dinner."

When they got back to Robbie's house, both Jamie and Melissa, came out to inspect Don's yellow beetle. Melissa liked the color. "Very flashy," she remarked. Jamie was surprised by how roomy it was and what the gas mileage was. "Don't you start getting ideas for one of these now," he said to Robbie.

"Dad," Robbie said, "not even if I get straight A's in all my classes throughout senior year like Donavon did? Because he did, you know."

"Tell you what, buddy, you get straight A's and I'll get you a Mustang."

"You heard him, Don. You're my witness. He just promised me a Mustang for graduation."

Everyone smiled and nodded their heads up and down. "Well, I got to go home now. Tomorrow's my first big day at work."

"Thanks for the ride to Sunrise Mountain today, Don. I really enjoyed it. If I don't see you sooner, I'll see you at six on July tenth for the party." His words of parting were, "Have fun with the Boy Scouts during the week. Don't let any of those little cubs drown."

The yellow beetle arrived at the Roberts' house at exactly six o'clock on July 10. Donavon noted that Cee jay's car was also parked in the driveway, so he pulled the beetle up next to it. Before getting out of the car, he gave the horn three "beep, beep, beeps.'

Donavon was in the mood for a pool party and was dressed for one. He was wearing his new solid scarlet board shorts. He had sneakers but no shirt; he had a large beach towel draped over his neck. He also carried a large box wrapped in colorful paper that had a picture of ducks quacking 'Happy Birthday.' An envelope was taped to the box.

Jamie opened the door before Donavon could ring the bell. He was surprised to see that Jamie also was dressed for a pool party. He was only wearing sandals and plaid board shorts.

"Donavon!" Jamie called his name so loud, he was surprised. "I just came in from the yard to get some plastic cups and heard you beeping. "Welcome! Welcome. Come on in. Robbie's up in his room changing. The rest of us are out in the back yard. I see that you are ready for the pool. Come on out."

"Thanks, Mr. Roberts, but if you don't mind, I'd first like to go up to Robbie's room to give him his." He indicated the box.

"Ah, I get it." He smiled and winked at Donavon. As he turned to walk away, he added. "Don, from now on, how about you just call me Jamie. Enough of that Mr. Roberts stuff. Okay?"

"Sure thing, Mr…er…Jamie."

"See ya later," he waved his hand as he walked toward the kitchen.

Before going up the stairs, Donavon paused to check out Jamie from the back. He was disappointed that Jamie wasn't wearing the speedos he had seen him in at the Manor. He also momentarily wondered if Dr. Seton would also be wearing the matching sexy bathing suit he had seen him in that night. Even though Jamie's bathing suit was not enticing to Don, he still thought the rest of him was. He liked his well-ribbed abs, pecks, strong muscular arms and back. Donavon also noticed that he had a particularly sexy walk.

Donavon knocked on Robbie's door. "Come on in, Don," Robbie called.

Opening the door, Donavon could see that Robbie was already in his bathing suit and a tee shirt with a picture of a bi-plane on the front. Just for a second, Donavon thought that he was looking at Jamie. Robbie resembled his father in many ways. He was Jamie's younger version, just as handsome, but leaner as a basketball player might be. Don instantly wanted to take him in his arms and hug him. "Ah, I'm glad you were up here because I wanted to give you this card and present in private," he said giving the box to Robbie.

"I guess I should open the card first." Both teenagers sat on the edge of Robbie's bed. The scent of Don's cologne was intoxicating as their thighs touched. Robbie laughed when he saw the picture on the front of the card. It showed a 747 jet flying through the clouds. It read: 'I wanted to buy you a ticket to an exotic place.' The inside message read: "But all I could afford was this cheap card. Happy Birthday, anyway." It was the written message under this that caused Robbie's emotions to rise. Donavon had written "from your 'blood-brother,' Don.'

"I like it when you think of me as your blood brother, Don. Thank you. Now let's see what's in this box." He slowly removed the wrapping paper. He had no idea what was in the box, but he knew it was from Don and that's all that really counted.

It was a kit for a model jet fighter. "This is the first jet I'll be making," he said. Suddenly, he remembered the plane he had made with Don, the one Don gave him and later he smashed and threw away in jealousy. He wondered if Donavon had noticed that it was missing from atop his bookcase.

"My parents gave me my birthday present this morning," Robbie said as he put the model kit on his desk. He picked up an envelope that sat there. He handed it to Don. "Look inside."

In the envelope was a birthday card and inside the card were two certificates for a pilot training program at Morristown Airport. "Gosh," Don said, "You really may be flying a plane before you get your driver's license. You must be really excited."

"I can hardly wait to start my lessons. I not only will be making model planes, I will be able to fly the real thing someday." Before sitting down on the bed again, he spread his arms, pretending they were wings of an airplane. He then gently put each hand on Donavon's ears. He bent in close to him and whispered, "And I want you to soar with me." He sat back down on the bed, so close that his hips and thighs were touching Donavon's.

"Ah, we have a party to get to downstairs," Don said.

"Yeah, we better not keep the gang wondering what's up with us. Let's go."

"Here's the birthday boy!" Jamie shouted as soon as the boys opened the sliding door onto the patio. Jamie's greeting was followed by cheers, applause, and some whistling from the guests.

A quick glance around the yard gave Robbie and Don a view of the guests. Bob Walsh and Susan Meeker were in the pool splashing one another. Roger Pucket was stretched out on a chaise lounge next to Judy Ferrero; they were holding hands. Three other members of the Mountain Ridge basketball team were standing by the pool talking to Barbie. Melissa was busy getting the table prepared for the buffet that would be put out shortly. Jamie was playing host and DJ at the make-shift "booth" on one side of the patio. Cee Jay was playing 'bartender' and 'chef.' He was wearing a chef's hat and apron and was trying to light the grill and make sure that the coolers were well stocked and everyone's plastic glass was always filled with soda or some other non-alcoholic beverage.

Don strolled over to join Barbie and the basketball players who had recently graduated. Robbie went to the chaise and poured a bottle of water on Roger who had his eyes closed. "You son-of-a-bitch!" Roger yelled at him and then started to laugh. "I'll get you for that." Robbie sat on the edge of Judy's chaise, and the three—now seniors—got into a lively discussion of the latest *Star Wars* movie.

Robbie's birthday party was a success. Everyone enjoyed jumping into the pool to play volleyball. The hot dogs and hamburgers–'la Seton'–the fixings, and side dishes were delicious. Jamie played some slow music that the guys and girls could dance arm in arm to. The teenagers particularly enjoyed seeing Jamie and Melissa dancing on the patio by themselves. After a while, Cee Jay cut in and started to dance with Melissa. Soon they were joined by Donavon and Barbie.

Later Jamie played a disco number that had all the teenagers on the dance 'floor' except Roger and Robbie who stood on the side watching. Eventually Judy grabbed Roger to join her, and Barbie pulled her brother to dance with her and Donavon. "It's okay to disco dance in threesomes, bro," Donavon said. "Just move to the music and let yourself go."

Robbie did just that. He soon began gyrating to whatever music Jamie played.

It was time to open the cards and gifts. Most of the cards were funny and received laughter as Robbie read each one. A big box that was from Roger contained a new basketball that had been signed by the entire team. Another box from Cee Jay contained a third certificate for a flying lesson at the Morristown Airport. The last gift to be opened was from Barbie. The box contained a complete outfit consisting of dress shoes, beige Docker slacks, and a Ben Hogan polo shirt. "I think your sister is trying to tell you something, dude," one of the basketball players joked.

Finally, it was dark enough to turn on the small Christmas lights that they always kept around the patio awning. Melissa and Cee Jay brought out a huge cake and ice cream. Jamie put eighteen candles into the whipped cream on the chocolate cake. Barbie led a chorus of the traditional singing of 'Happy Birthday.' It was Roger who yelled out, "Make a wish before blowing out the candles."

Robbie looked around at all his guest. He seemed to give Cee Jay a special, quick smile. His big smile resembled that of a cat that just swallowed the canary. He inhaled deeply and then blew out all eighteen candles.

Chapter 22

DURING THE FOLLOWING WEEK Donavon called Robbie to ask him if he would like to go to the Boy Scout Day Camp with him on Sunday. He told him that his first week as head swimming instructor had gone very well and he was enjoying his job. The young scouts were enthusiastic and willing to learn to swim. He told Robbie that on Sunday, they would have the whole camp to themselves for boating, swimming, or playing any of the games the camp has."

Of course, Robbie quickly said yes. Don told him that he would pick him up at his house at one o'clock. He reminded Robbie to bring his camera, drinking water, and sun screen. "Let's hope it doesn't rain; but even if it does, we can hang out in the dining hall and play games. I'm anxious to show you the place, Roberts. It will be lots of fun."

Fortunately, the day was beautiful. It was a perfect day for being on a lake at a camp which the teens would have all to themselves. Robbie relayed his excitement to his mom and dad as Melissa prepared a lunch of a few sandwiches, peaches, bananas, and two bottles of Sunny D for them.

Robbie had his bathing suit and a tee shirt on but had put underwear and shorts as well as a towel in his big, red gym bag along with the food stuff his mom had prepared. He was really psyched when at one o'clock he heard Don's 'beep, beep, beep' outside.

Donavon greeted him with a fist knock, Robbie threw his gym bag on the back seat, and they were off to Culvers Lake.

The Boy Scout Day Camp was not easy to find if you didn't know of its existence. There was only a small sign announcing it on the county road. The road leading to the camp itself was gravel. A heavy growth of pine and other trees and bushes protected it. A chain link fence that stood about six feet high surrounded the entire site on the land side. Donavon explained that the fence was there to protect the camp from vagabonds, but mostly from the bears, deer, and coyotes who were known to inhabit the area. "Smaller critters like rabbits and mice manage to squeeze in, however. Just yesterday we found a skunk in reception," he said. Don laughed. "That skunk put up quite a stink when we wouldn't let him stay."

Donavon gave a key to Robbie to open the pad lock and gate. He told him to lock it again once he was within the compound. Beyond the gate, the gravel road turned to the left. Donavon parked the yellow beetle in front of a building that had a sign saying "Welcome: Camp Reception."

"Come on. I'll show you around before we go into the lake," Donavon said. He lead Robbie into the small reception cabin which contained a counter and the office of the director.

The walls were filled with cork boards on which activities schedules, camp rules and regulations, and many Boy Scout notices were posted. "The boys don't want to be sent here," Donavon said. "It's like being sent to the principal's office in a school."

Opposite the reception cabin was a larger building which was the game room and dining hall. Another large room off the game area was used for instructional purposes and different meetings. A cafeteria style counter was at one end of the dining area. Don briefly turned on the light in the kitchen to point out the stoves, ovens, and refrigerators. "Once a week, chef makes pizza for the boys. That's the one meal they all like the most, but he prepares really good, nutritious lunches every day," Donavon said.

The next building on the short tour contained the lockers, showers, and restroom facilities. "The boys are expected to attend the camp in their uniforms and to change here. They must bring their own towels and either buy a combination lock here or bring one from home," Don explained. "One problem that we have is that there are not enough lockers for each boy to have his own assigned locker. They can't keep anything here over night. So, each day it becomes a first-come -first served scramble to get a locker."

The last building in the compound was opposite the changing cabin. "This building is for the counselors," Donavon said unlocking the door. Inside were four tables with chairs at each. On both sides of the room were small offices for each of the three counselors. Don pointed out the one that was his. The door to it had a sign that read "Don Rice, Life Guard and Swim Instructor." In his small office, there was room only for a small desk and chair, two small arm chairs, and a fairly large, black file cabinet. "I keep files on each boy's swimming level and progress and what water activities he engages in," Donavon proudly announced to Robbie.

The building was divided by a hall at one end. A door on one side had a sign saying "Men's Restroom." The door on the opposite side announced the "Men's Lockers and Showers."

Back outside, Don showed the small sand area that was the camp beach, his life guard stand, and a wooden pier to which two row boats were moored. Don pointed out the large wooden raft in the middle of the cove. Robbie estimated that the raft was about 150 feet from the beach and the cove extended about another 150 feet on each side of the raft. The land on both sides, which also extended about another 100 feet from the raft was densely covered with trees and bushes, making the area very private except where the cove opened to Culvers Lake itself. "Well, that's it for the tour," Donavon said. "Any questions? Comments?"

"The camp is much bigger than I thought when I saw it from Sunrise Mountain," Robbie said. "Do you know how deep the water is out at the raft?"

"Yes, at the raft, it's twelve feet. See the roped-off area. I keep the boys within the ropes on either side because its clean mud and sand. At the ropes, it's five feet deep. We have races to the raft and back, but the races are only for the older boys who have past my swimming and safety test. One of my goals for this season is that every boy learns to swim and can at least make it to the raft and back again. A lot of the bigger boys like to hang out around the raft. They can jump off it, but I don't allow any rough housing."

Don led the way back to the counselors' cabin. "Let's change into our swim trunks now and take one of the row boats out on the lake. By the way, power boats are not permitted on the lake. Culvers is not like Mohawk, which is noisy and dangerous because of the speed boats and water skiers. Culvers is very quiet and private. Personally, I prefer Culvers over Lake Mohawk and High Point, but there's certainly more to do and see at those lakes."

Donavon had his own locker in the changing room. He told Robbie to take a locker at the far end and proceeded to quickly undress and change into his bathing suit. Robbie took longer to take off his sneakers, undress and change because he wanted to catch a glimpse of Don naked. Unfortunately, however, Don removed his briefs and slipped into his bathing suit before removing his tee shirt. He never removed his sandals. "Did you bring sun glasses?" he asked.

"Damn. I forgot."

"No worries. I always have an extra pair for a kid who needs them. Take these," he said giving a pair to Robbie. "There may be a glare on the lake. You may also want your sun lotion and camera."

"Yes, mother," Robbie said sarcastically while putting on the glasses.

Don put on a muscle tee that said "Lifeguard." Robbie noticed that the same thing was written in the front of one side of Don's bathing suit.

Outside, Donavon opened a large storage box, which contained, among other things, the row boat oars. "You can row while we're in the cove," Don said while putting the oars in their locks. Robbie situated himself in the boat as Don untied it from the pier. He gently pushed the boat away before getting into it himself. "Okay, Captain Roberts, let's get this ship moving," he said.

"Aye, aye, sailor," Robbie joked back.

It took little adjustment for Robbie to master rowing the large boat, which he felt could easily hold six passengers. Donavon sat at the bow and occasionally gave a suggestion to "give it more on the left or right" but mostly kept his eyes on Robbie. It didn't take long to get to the buoy which marked the entrance to the cove. At this point, Donavon took over the job of rowing, while Robbie carefully moved to the seat that Don had occupied.

Robbie put his hand into the water. "It's icy," he said.

"Yeah. It tends to warm up as the summer progresses, but generally it is colder out here on the lake than in the cove. Later, when we are in the middle, if you put your hand in the water, you may actually feel a current. The lake is fed by a few streams but mostly by natural springs."

"You seem to know a lot about the lake," Robbie said.

"Well, I've been coming here for many years. First as a cub scout and for the last two years as a counselor. Now as life guard. I really like the camp and the lake."

"Do you know how deep it is?"

"Not really. I've heard a variety of depths. Kind'a dependents on who you're taking to. I've heard anywhere from fifty feet to a hundred. My guess would be around fifty, though." He paused while Robbie took a picture of him.

"I'll take you past a few of the big waterfront houses before we head to the other side."

"Do you know anyone who lives in the houses?" Robbie asked.

"No. Most of the big homes are occupied only in the summer months. Rich people come here. They're mostly out-of-staters. The water front homes are very expensive. The land that the camp is on was willed to the Boy Scouts by a rich U.S. Senator."

Robbie was enjoying the warm sun on his body. He took several pictures of the lake and another one of Donavon. He liked looking at Don's strong arms and muscles. "Why don't you take your shirt off so I can get a picture of your Charles Atlas chest," he said.

Donavon needed no encouraging; he almost immediately put the oars up and striped off his muscle-tee. "Happy now?" he said.

Robbie focused his camera, but as he was snapping the shutter, Don stuck his tongue out. "That's something my dad would do," he chuckled. "Now be serious and I'll take another one."

For the second picture, Donavon didn't stick his tongue out but did look very, very serious, almost as if he were going to cry. "You're worse than my dad. Now, will you just smile like a normal human being?"

"Yessum, master, if I can then take a picture of you."

Robbie got the picture he wanted and gave the camera to Donavon who shot two pictures of Robbie; one was a full frontal, the other a side view.

"You better put some lotion on before you start to burn," Donavon instructed.

While the row boat just drifted in the middle of the lake, Robbie rubbed the sun tan lotion over his face, arms, legs and chest. He handed the tube to Don. "Put some on my back," he said.

"Ah, ah."

"Please," Robbie said.

"Okay." Don padded the seat and moved over, leaving room for Robbie. "Be careful."

"That feels good," Robbie said as Donavon smeared the lotion on his back. Actually, it felt awesome as Don's hands moved gently over his back. So awesome, Robbie felt it in his penis which began to express his emotion. He became embarrassed. He took the tube from Don. "Now let me do a smear job on your back."

Don turned sideways so Robbie could put the lotion on his back. Robbie loved the excitement touching Donavon's back gave him. It was like an electric charge that caressed his entire body. Involuntarily, his penis also reacted again and Robbie felt the wetness of pre-cum in his bathing suit. He wanted to continue to rub Don's back. He longed to reach over and run his hands over Don's rippled chest. He was urged to touch his nipples with his fingers. But this may have led to a full boner on his part and a big embarrassment for both of them.

"Hey, you better not breath a word of this to Pucket," Don said suddenly.

That was what Robbie needed to hear to get him back to reality, but it also told him that Donavon was thinking something pretty close to what he himself was thinking. "My lips are sealed," he said reassuringly and handed the lotion back to Don. "You can put some on your own face and arms." He carefully moved back to his position at the bow.

"Thanks," Don responded. He put lotion on the rest of his body as Robbie looked on admiringly. He tossed the tube back to Robbie and started rowing to the other side. Neither boy spoke for several minutes. Each was trying to guess what the other was thinking.

Don rowed past the buoy on the shore opposite the cove before slowly navigating the boat in a wide turn to head back to the camp. Robbie used his zoom lens to take a few pictures at both ends of the lake. The conversation back to the day camp was largely about Donavon's hopes for playing football at Rutgers and his insecurities of getting to be a quarterback on the outstanding Scarlet team. He knew that he had to prove himself against some of the best talents in the state. He had done well during the last two years, but he would now only be a freshman and facing a lot of competition. "If I do pursue a duel major, I don't know if I can keep up with all the classes, studies, and play football at the same time," Don confessed. "Frankly, I'm scared."

"Well, give it your best for at least a year," Robbie said. "Remember: it's only a game. Your studies may determine your entire career and life. Besides, there are too many serious injuries you can suffer in football. I would really hate to see you seriously hurt, Don."

"Thanks for the advice. I'll keep it in mind."

They docked the boat and immediately started romping in the water. They splashed one another. Leg grabbed one another. They wrestled. Donavon made the challenge that they swim out to raft.

Don got to the raft first, but Robbie wasn't far behind. Hanging on to the edge of the raft Robbie looked up into the eyes of Donavon who was sitting on it. "You beat me only because you've been practicing all week. I haven't been in the water since last summer," Robbie said shaking the water out of his hair.

"Roberts you couldn't beat me if you swam every day. Remember. I'm the life guard," Don retorted. He extended his hand to Robbie to help pull him onto the raft.

Both teenagers sat side by side with their feet tangling in the cool water of the cove.

After a while, Robbie said, "This sure is nice. Being here with you, I mean."

Donavon put his hand on Robbie's shoulder. "It sure is…It sure is, blood brother."

Robbie remembered the model air plane and suddenly felt guilty for having broken it and throwing it away; but he was glad his hero remembered the incident.

Donavon stretched out on his back; he put his hands under his head to act as a pillow against the hard, wooden raft.. Robbie, who was still seated, looked down at Donavon. His eyes immediately saw Don's crotch, then his belly button just peeking over Don's suit, and then his enticing chest. Robbie yearned to touch him. He desperately wanted to lay on top of him, just to have their bodies connect. If only he knew how to do it…could do it.

A minute passed before Robbie said, "It was nice of your grandparents to give you the yellow beetle for graduation."

"Yeah. They said it was also for my birthday, but I bet they'll send me a gift—probably a check—for that too. Hey, did you speak to Barbie and your mom and dad about having a duel birthday party and a going away to college party?"

"Yeah, they liked the idea, but said that it should be on Barbie's birthday, which also happens to be a Saturday, a better day for a party. So if you don't mind celebrating your birthday a few days early, were all set."

"That's great, Robbie. I don't mind having a party a few days before my actual birthday."

"I hope my dad behaves himself at the party. You don't know how silly my dad can get. My mom said that after you guys left the graduation party at Cee Jay's man cave, he became an embarrassment. I was in the other room watching baseball on television so I didn't see him, but mom said he was telling jokes and doing some of his crazy karaoke routines. He started disco dancing with Dr. Jorgensen. Mom said that she thought he had too much to drink and insisted that she drive the car home."

"Well, I like your dad, Robbie. He's easy to talk to and a lot of fun to be around. I wish he were my dad, rather than that meat head step-father of mine. Robbie, between you and me, I can't stand that fucking guy. I'll be glad to go to college, just to get away from him."

"Wow. What's wrong with him?"

"I don't know why my mom ever married him. He's fat, ugly, and a slob for starters. He treats my mom like a servant and never says anything nice to her. He moved into our house ten years ago, and I don't think I've ever had a decent conversation with him. He acts as though he owns the house. When my dad died, he left the house to me and my mother. My mother is a saint for putting up with him." He sat up again and looked directly at Robbie.

"I was only six when my real dad died. My mom took his sudden death very badly. My grandparents did also because he was their only child. Two years later when grandpa Rice retired, they moved down to Florida. Mom tried to do all she could for me, but I know it must have been difficult. She took me down to Florida for about two weeks; and shortly after we got back, she got married. I think the purpose for our going to Florida was to get advice and consent from my grandparents for her to remarry. You know…that old crap about 'the boy needs a father' shit. Since then I think my grandparents have been spoiling me. We talk on the phone a lot, but I really miss having them live near-by."

Donavon chuckled, "Who the hell would ever leave Sussex County to go to Boca Raton, Florida?"

After a long pause, Donavon said, "Let's get back to land, shower and change into dry clothes. I want to play a game of chess with you before we leave. Okay?"

Robbie nodded his head in agreement, and Don said, "This time I'll let you beat me in a race to the beach."

Back in the counselors' cabin, Robbie followed Donavon's lead by going directly into the shower room. He also followed Donavon's lead by not taking his bathing suit off. They stood opposite one another in the room. Shortly, the water got too cold. Robbie turned it off and took the lead in taking his trunks off. Donavon followed, but turned his back to face the wall as he took his bathing suit off. Both teenagers started to put soap on their bodies.

Donavon turned to look at Robbie who still had his back to him. He had never seen Robbie completely naked before. He suddenly felt an urge to touch his back. To run his hands over Robbie's cute ass. Robbie was so innocent. So loving.

"Hey, let me wash your back," Donavon suddenly said.

Robbie handed Don his bar of soap.

Without hesitation, Don took the soap and began rubbing it on his friend. Instantly, Donavon began to realize he was getting a hard-on. Robbie turned slightly and saw that his penis was also getting larger. Donavon lost himself in touching Robbie's back. Suddenly, Donavon realized that he wanted him. He wrapped his hand around Robbie's chest. Still with the soap in his hand, he instinctively grabbed Robbie's penis. Robbie said nothing. Donavon was lost in the pleasure.

Don dropped the soap onto the shower floor. Both were now fully erect. Donavon continued to massage Robbie's penis. He turned Robbie toward him so their cocks touched. He nearly burst. He grabbed both cocks and began rubbing both together. Robbie seemed to go limp. Donavon grabbed him with his other arm. Robbie turned the water back on. He leaned against the wall and watched it pour over their cocks.

This was not a time to think about it; he had done enough thinking. Now he wanted it. Don fell to his knees and put Robbie's beautiful engorged member in his mouth and at the same time began fondling his own. He felt himself having an orgasm at the same moment Robbie yelled out and pulled away from Donavon.

Robbie's load landed on the floor, while Donavon came all over Robbie's legs and feet. Both boys were stunned, shocked, and didn't know if their shivering was caused by their own nervousness or the effect of what they both had done or the chill that they both felt.

Donavon got up from the cold, wet floor and began immediately to wash off the last drops of his semen. He could not speak.

Robbie felt exhausted; he had to steady himself by turning on the water and holding onto the faucet to gain his equilibrium. Although he had wanted to have this experience, it was not how he wanted it to happen. It took him by total surprise, and it was too quick. He definitely ejaculated too quickly. There didn't seem to be any emotion in their act. The whole sex thing must have taken only a few minutes. But it was a glorious moment that he wanted to repeat and repeat and repeat again with Donavon.

Donavon turned his shower off. "We better get going," he said sheepishly. He seemed to run into the locker room. Robbie was still stunned by the experience. The cold water helped to bring him to his senses, and shortly he turned off the shower and went into the locker room to dry off and get dressed.

Both teens were silent as Donavon quickly got fully dressed. Robbie was tying the laces on his sneakers when Donavon finally spoke. "What just happened in there, never happened, Roberts. Remember, it never happened. Forget it!" He said angrily.

Robbie was hurt. He thought: *Of course, it happened. How could he deny it? Why did Don now seem so angry? He's the one who started it. Why does he seem to be in such a state of denial?*

Donavon was ashamed of himself. *I should have had better control. I didn't know what I was thinking. I had no right to start that with him. What if he reports it to his father or to the Boy*

Scouts? Or Walsh? I really like Robbie, but I should never have gone down on him.

As they were leaving the counselors' cabin, Don handed the gate keys to Robbie. "Please make sure the gate is closed and locked," was the only thing he said while walking back to the Volkswagen.

After Robbie got back into the car, Donavon turned directly to him. "I'm sorry I started what happened in the shower. Please try to forget it. I promise it will never happen again."

Robbie was too choked up by his own emotions to answer. Both remained silent as they left Culvers Lake and headed back to Robbie's house.

Getting out of the yellow beetle, Robbie turned to Donavon. "You may be sorry that it happened, but I'm not, Don." He emphasized the word 'not.' "It did happen, and I'm glad it did, so don't deny it; but don't worry. Your dirty little secret will stay with me only.' He paused. "Goodbye."

To Donavon that "goodbye" meant that he would never see Robbie again.

Chapter 23

THE INCIDENT AT THE Boy Scout Day Camp left Robbie Roberts completely distraught. He absolutely could not understand Donavon Rice's reactions. They had been having a great time until that happened. But what was it that actually did happen? Suddenly, Don had started washing his back, then yanking at his cock, then sucking his cock. It was wild and bizarre. He had never had anyone do that to him. It was crazy, but he had to admit that he liked it. He would do it again if Donavon wanted. But what caused Donavon to do it all of a sudden? Did Donavon like it? Would Donavon want to do it again? Or would he "forget that it ever happened"?

Robbie knew that he only would do something like that with Don. He certainly wouldn't even think of doing it with any other guy he ever knew. Yes, all that afternoon, he wanted to touch Donavon, be very close to him. But having him rub their cocks together and then to get on his knees like that had to be weirder than weird. Had Donavon ever done anything like that with any other guy? Did he hate Robbie for being the object of his lust? Did Don get mad that he didn't tell him how good it felt at the time?

Cee Jay had asked Robbie if Donavon had ever attempted anything like that. Now he could say 'yes.' Did that make Donavon a pervert or gay? Certainly, after both of them ejaculated, Robbie wouldn't say that either he or Don were now gay. At first, Robbie wanted to run to Cee Jay to tell him what had happened and Don's silent mood afterward, but he had promised Donavon that he would not tell anyone about his 'secret.' Now, however, he realized that it was 'their' secret. By not fighting Don off, would Don now think that Robbie was gay?

Now, Cee Jay was unavailable; he was thousands of miles away in southern Spain.

Robbie still couldn't talk to his father about the incident. He almost knew that if he told Jamie about it, Jamie would probably say something stupid like "Did he wear a condom?" or "He probably just lost his head for a moment" or "You should start looking for another boyfriend." Were these the kinds of things a bi-sexual like his dad would say? Robbie himself had thought of these responses and had to reject all of them. The only thing that Robbie could do was to grin and bear it in silence by himself. He realized, however, it would not be easy.

He tried hanging out with Pucket more. He even called Bob Walsh to suggest they go bike riding or take a ride to High Point or Sunrise Mountain. Walsh did opt for a day at the lake at High Point. While there, Robbie asked if Walsh had seen Donavon. Walsh told him that he had not seen or heard from him since his birthday party. "I guess he's busy working at his day camp during the week and at Mickey D's on weekends. Now that he has his own car, he might be dating every girl in school. It's strange though that he hasn't called me or answered my telephone messages. Do you know if Barbie's seen him?"

Robbie knew that if Barbie had seen or heard from Don within the last three weeks that he and all the Roberts family would have known about it.

A few days later, when he was in the park with Roger, Pucket casually said, "Hey, I ran into Don Rice after church yesterday."

"Really? What did he have to say?"

"Not too much. Just that he was looking forward to going to Rutgers. He did ask if I I'd seen you. When I told him that, yeah, you and I were shooting hoops and riding our bikes a lot, he said 'Good.' Tell Robbie I said 'Hello.'"

It wasn't much, but at least Robbie knew that Donavon was still thinking of him, and by talking to Pucket, he could guess that Robbie never told him about the 'incident.' Robbie thought of calling Donavon, but since he wasn't talking to Bob Walsh, his best friend, he certainly wouldn't want to talk to him. Besides, Robbie wouldn't know what to say. How could he even broach the subject, let alone explain fully all the feelings he had been having for him.

One day, Robbie sat at his bedroom desk and cried. He had looked at the three pictures he saved in his digital camera of Donavon the night of the prom. He thought of the fact that he had jerked off for the first time thinking about Donavon that night. He looked at the pictures he had taken at Culvers Lake. Among them, he was puzzled by one that showed a close-up of Robbie's crotch. Did Donavon deliberately snap this picture? Was it supposed to be a joke? Did he himself accidentally take it? Robbie wondered why, if Donavon had taken it, why did he? Was he thinking of Robbie sexually all that afternoon as he was of Don? Perhaps that incident in the shower had been on Donavon's mind for some time.

Another week passed. One evening Jamie and Robbie were playing one-on-one in the driveway, when Jamie said, "Donavon Rice gave me a call at the office today."

Robbie was stunned. "Why? Why did he call you?" What did he have to say?"

Jamie stopped dribbling the basketball. "Well, it was rather strange. He wanted to know if the party for your sister's birthday was still on. I told him that we would also celebrate his birthday and I was under the impression that we would also think of it as a going away party for Barbie, himself, Bob Walsh, and whomever else they wanted to invite from their class."

"What else did he say, dad?"

"mmm. Nothing except if I heard how Cee Jay was doing in Spain. I told him that Cee Jay would be home for the party."

"Did Donavon say anything else? Did he mention me at all? You know, I haven't seen or spoken to him in several weeks. Not since the time we went to the camp at Culvers lake."

"No, that was it." Jamie dribbled the basketball and took a jump for a perfect two-pointer shot.

That night Robbie looked at his pictures of Donavon again. He was glad that he had not deleted any of the pictures from Culvers Lake.

One evening the following week, the telephone rang. As usual, Melissa answered. Robbie could hear her talking to someone but couldn't make out any of the conversation. He was pleasantly surprised, however, when she yelled up the stairs, "Robbie, I have Donavon on the phone. He wants to talk to you."

"Okay, mom. Tell him I'll be right there." He bounded down the stairs and took the phone from her. Melissa handed him the phone and went into the kitchen.

"Hello." Robbie said softly.

"Roberts, I have to talk to you."

"About the party? Dad said he told you it was definitely a go."

"No, it's not about the party. I have to talk to you about something else. I think you know what it's about."

"Yes, I do." Robbie paused. "So, I'm listening."

"I really don't want to talk about it on the telephone. Is it okay if we get together this Saturday? I'm not working until six, so we could go to High Point or someplace to talk privately."

"I'm game for that, Don."

"Awesome! I was afraid you might not want to talk to me. I'll pick you up at your house at 10 on Saturday then."

"Okay. Bye."

"And, Robbie, thanks," Donavon said in ending.

Melissa came back into the living room. "So, are you and Don going to do something?" she asked.

"Yeah, he wants me to go up to High Point with him on Saturday."

"That's nice," Melissa said. "He's a good boy. He must be busy these days. He hasn't been around in a while."

Robbie was ready and waiting outside when the yellow beetle pulled in the Roberts driveway. He got into the car immediately.

"Hi, Roberts."

"Hi, Don."

Donavon put the beetle in gear and they drove off.

It was Robbie who broke the awkward silence between them. "I'm glad you called me, Don. I've been going crazy wondering about you."

"Well, your father deserves the credit for motivating me to call you. I probably wouldn't have, if it were not for him."

Robbie gulped. "You spoke to my dad about the shower incident?"

"Yes."

"Oh, my God! You told my dad? What did he say?"

"He told me to call you and to discuss the whole thing with you. He promised not to talk to you about it until I spoke to you first. He said that he would go along with anything that you would say, and that I should also accept anything you said. Your dad is an easy man to talk to, Robbie. I had no one to confide in and I was really confused. At Culvers that day I told you how much I admired your dad and how lucky you were to have a guy like him as a father."

"What should I say…What can I say…about what happened?"

Neither boy spoke for some time.

"Robbie, I'm terribly sorry about that incident in the shower. It should never have happened. I lost my head. I guess I was just thinking through my dick and got carried away. I want you to know that I never did anything like that before in my life. Remember when I told you I was a virgin? Well, I am. With girls as well as guys. I swear to God, Robbie, that was the first time. I don't know what caused me to lose it in the shower."

"It was a first for me too, Don; and in case you hadn't noticed, I had a boner and got off too."

"I know that, Robbie. That's why I hope I haven't harmed you in any way. Emotionally, I mean." He paused. "Robbie, I'm not gay!"

"Neither am I, Don. But I have kind of thought about you that way."

"What do you mean 'that way'?"

"You know…sexually. It was all too sudden; I wasn't prepared for it and certainly didn't want it to happen the way it did."

"When you got out of the car that afternoon, you said that you were glad it happened. Why?"

"Because deep down, I guess I wanted it to happen. I wanted to know if you felt the same way about me as I did you. At first, I thought 'Yes, he does.' But then you got angry and started saying crazy things, but never told me why. And then for weeks you haven't called or anything. That's the part that hurts the most, Don. And now you're telling me that you're not gay.

I may be only an eighteen-year old virgin, but I'd say any guy who does what you did, was gay. And I went along with it, and I admit: I enjoyed it. If you wanted to, I'd do it again. Maybe a lot differently, but I would. Does that make me gay? So be it, I'm gay. What the hell is that any way? Gay! I swear, Don, I never thought about any guy the way I thought about you, think about anyone else now, or even think I ever would with any dude. Gay! Hell, it's just a fucking word. But, yeah, I liked it. I came all over the floor, didn't I? And you came all over my feet and legs. Does that make us gay? I don't know, and I don't care. It was something we shared, and that's that."

They had arrived at the state park. Don opted to pay the fee up to the obelisk monument rather than the beach, which cost more. He parked his car as far away from the few other cars in the lot as possible. "I guess everyone is either in the picnic area or at the lake," he commented. "Have you ever gone to the top of the obelisk? The view is spectacular even from here, but up on top you can actually see all three states: New Jersey, New York, and Pennsylvania."

"I thought we were going swimming," Robbie said.

"Oh, my bad," Don answered. "I should have told you. The lake and beach will probably be very crowded now. Too crowded for us to talk privately. Why don't we just sit over there on one of those benches, and talk. If you want, later we can hike up the steps to the top of the monument. Maybe some other day we can do the lake. Right now, I think being in a locker room or shower with you would be too dangerous.

"When did you start thinking about me...er, us...like that, Roberts?"

"The night at the Manor, when you hugged me outside my room."

"Wow! Really? That was the same day I met you." He paused. "I have a confession now to make to you. I started to think about you even before that. Walsh and I were at a game last year, and he pointed you out. That was it for me. Yep, that's when I first started getting the hots for you, Roberts."

"You're kidding, right? You felt that way too! Why didn't you say something or do something?"

"Yeah, sure." Donavon gestured with his fingers and hands. "Can you just see the headlines: 'Senior quarterback tells junior basketball star he's in love with him.' Because I was, you know…in love with you…Still am."

"Oh, my God!" Robbie turned on the park bench, faced Don, and put both arms around him in the tightest bear hug imaginable. "You have no idea how happy it makes me to know that. I can kiss you right here and now."

"Ah. Better not do that right here, buddy. There may be some reporters around. And you know what Dr. Seton would say: "Teenage ost…"

Robbie finished the sentence with him. "Ostentatious display of affection." Both boys chuckled and began crying at the same time.

Using the back of his hands to wipe away tears, Robbie said, "I have another confession to make. Remember the night of your prom. When I was taking pictures, I took three pictures just of you."

"Ah, I remember that. I thought you were."

"Yeah, but that night I jerked off looking at them."

Donavon gave Robbie a jab with his elbow. "Why, you dirty little pervert!"

"Yeah, but look who's calling me a pervert. The guy who gives another dude a blow job on his knees in a Boy Scout shower room." They both laughed.

"But who got that pervert all hot and bothered all day by taking all kinds of pictures and making innuendos so that he went crazy?"

"I confess. That was me. I'm guilty." Both boys were deep in thought. Robbie finally broke the silence between them. "So where do we go from here, Mr. Donavon Rice?"

When Donavon spoke, he was very serious. "Roberts, a few minutes ago you said you would do it again, but differently. What did you mean: differently?"

"I would want to make love to you. You know, love. Not just some quick jerk off. I'd want it to be romantic."

"Romantic. How?" Donavon asked. "Do you mean flowers and music and stuff?"

"mmm…Not really. But that does sort of give one fantasies. I was thinking more in the line of kissing. I hear that you're a great kisser."

"Kissing, huh." Donavon smiled. "I can do kissing. What else?"

"Touching. I'd love to touch you all over. Feel those strong abs. I've fantasized thinking about running my hands through your hair. Sucking on your earlobes and your nipples. Feeling your body against mine. Maybe taking your cock in my mouth. I'd love to taste your cum. The thought of your stiff cock against my ass has caused me to jerk off."

"Okay. Okay. I get the picture. Wow! You certainly can get a guy hot. I'm getting wet just listening to you. I promise, next time I'll be much better. More romantic."

"So, will I. So, will I," Robbie repeated thoughtfully. "And it will just be something between us alone. The hell with anyone else who wants to put labels on what we feel for one another. "

"Great!" Donavon said. "Now let's climb up to the top of the monument."

Chapter 24

WHEN DONAVON AND ROBBIE got back from High Point State Park, they were surprised to see both Cee Jay and Jamie in the driveway checking out Cee Jay's car. Jamie had gone to Cee Jay's house a few times to make sure that everything in the house was in good order, to bring in the mail, and start up the car. He occasionally went to the kennel to visit Checkers to make sure the dog was doing well and to be petted by a familiar human. Cee Jay had brought a basket filled with Spanish wines for Jamie and Melissa. As they were shaking hands and welcoming home the teacher, Donavon thought that his former teacher looked healthier and more relaxed. He had a golden tan and seemed a few pounds thinner. He also now knew the complete story of the relationship between Jamie and Cee Jay.

"So, I'm glad to see that you two boys are still hanging out together," Cee Jay said. "Have you been having a good summer?"

"We did have a few problems, but we've been working on them," Don said. "Yes, I guess we had an interesting summer so far. We just came back from High Point. We climbed all the way to the top of the monument for that magnificent view."

"It's one of my favorite spots in the state," Cee Jay said. "I don't know why I went all the way to Malaga, when we have such beauty right here in our own back yard." He turned to directly address Don. "How is that yellow VW of yours, Donavon?"

"Fine sir, fine. I haven't been using it as much as I would like, but it gets me to my Culvers Lake job as well as the one at MacDonald's. I'll be driving down to New Brunswick in a few weeks, so it will get a real work out then."

"I envy you for just starting college, Donavon. I wish I had those days to live over. They were very exciting. College will open a new world for you. New experiences. New opportunities. Take advantage of them."

"Yes, sir. *Carpe diem*. That's what you taught us."

"Good, boy. Now let's talk about that party Jamie has said you are having. I understand that you and Barbie are celebrating your birthdays, which are just a few days apart; and you also want us all to cry because you're leaving us for college. It's all a great idea."

Cee Jay added, "I'll help out with the decorations, Melissa will provide the food, and Jamie will supply…Jamie, what is it you're contributing again?…Oh, yes, your questionable talents as singer and DJ. I'll make sure he isn't too embarrassing." He said this while putting both arms around Jamie's shoulders and shaking him. "We all think this is going to a great party anyway, don't you?"

"Sounds good," Donavon said and Robbie nodded his head in agreement.

"How about a start time around four o'clock," Jamie said. "That way you can party well into the night if you like. I'll make sure that the pool is clean and working properly, so you can tell all your friends to bring bathing suits if they want."

"Awesome." Donavon said.

"It's all settled then. You can start sending out the invitations. I need to be heading home to take care of my four-legged pal. Will I being seeing you later, Jamie?"

"Sure, if you make that paella you were raving about before."

"Will do. So long, guys. I'll see you guys at the party, if not sooner. Later, Jamie." Before starting the car, Cee Jay reached out to grab Robbie's hand. "Robbie, call me if you want to discuss anything."

"Thanks, Dr. S." He turned to give a quick glance to Donavon before adding with a smile, "but I don't think that will be necessary."

"Good, I was hoping that you'd say that. So long now."

The yellow beetle arrived at the Roberts' house at four o'clock on August 19th. Donavon noted that Cee Jay's car was parked in the driveway, so he pulled the beetle up next to it. Before getting out of the car, he gave his customary three 'Beep, Beep, Beeps.'

Donavon was carrying a box wrapped in heavy gold foil. Barbie opened the door for him. She gave him a hug and kissed him on the cheek. "Happy birthday, Don. You know, if I were born here rather than in Brooklyn, we may have shared nursery cribs." They both chuckled.

"Hey, are you ready for Middlebury?"

"Just about. I'm still packing. I need to take enough stuff until I get back to New Jersey in December. My dad's pick-up is going to be packed."

"Robbie tells me you decided to stay in Jersey and go to Rutgers."

"Yeah, you can't take me out of the 'Garden State,' but I'll be in New Brunswick, far enough away from my family to make it an adventure."

"We will have to get together during Christmas break. Please keep in touch, Donavon. You were one of my least chauvinistic classmates." She smiled. "Seriously, though, I did enjoy our times together, particularly our senior English project and, of course, the prom." She gently took hold of his arm to lead him. "Everyone is out back."

"Is Robbie upstairs? I have something here that I'd like to give him before the party."

She spotted the foil wrapped box in his hand. "Oh, sure. Go on up. I think he was waiting for you." She winked. "I think that he has a little present for you too."

"Ah, I'm glad you were up here because I wanted to give you this in private," he said handing the box to Robbie.

"Hey, my birthday was last month, but I'll take a present any time. This is really wrapped beautifully." He then handed a nicely wrapped gift to Donavon. "Since this is your birthday, though, I think you should open this gift first."

Robbie's present was a dual-hinged, heavy wooden picture frame. One side contained a close-up of Robbie rowing the boat at Culvers lake. On the other side was a picture of Donavon at Sunrise Mountain. In the box with the two framed pictures, Robbie also enclosed a $25. Wal Mart gift certificate. Donavon swore that he would always keep the pictures on his dorm desk.

"I know your birthday was last month, but a lot has happened between us since then, and I want you to have this."

The expression on Robbie's face indicated bewilderment. He slowly began to undo the wrapping.

"Go on, open it."

Robbie was speechless. Inside was a thin gold chain and a gold friendship ring with a black leather thin trim. An engraving inside the ring read "Robbie & Don."

"Put it on."

The ring slide perfectly on his finger. "How did you know what my size was?"

"I didn't. Your father told me. I told your dad what I wanted to get you, and he actually went to the jewelry store in Morristown with me to help pick it out. I swear, Roberts. your dad is the greatest guy I know."

"Donavon, it's gorgeous! I love it. And I love you." Without hesitation, he kissed Don on the lips. Suddenly, both boys realized that finally they were having their first kiss. It wasn't awkward or embarrassing. They both experienced a joy beyond their understanding. Momentarily they paused to look directly into one another's eyes. Then Donavon initiated another kiss. This one was long, gentle, and filled with magic. Both boys lost themselves in the warmth of one another's breathe.

Instinctively, Donavon pulled Robbie down on the bed aside himself. Their tongues touched and teased. Donavon reached under Robbie's tee. He ran his hands over Robbie's smooth back. Robbie wrapped both hands around Donavon to lock their bodies together. Robbie felt Don's strong back and ran his hand over his arm muscles. He moved slightly to get his hand on Don's chest and continue to kiss. Both young men realized that their dicks were erect within their swim suits. Their hearts were pounding. Donavon reached down and rubbed Robbie's erection through the swim suit.

"Ah, let's not get too carried away here," Robbie said softly while trying to control his own desires. "We have a party to get to downstairs. My mom probably will be banging on the door any second now."

"Damn, and we were just starting with our own party here," Donavon chuckled. He got off the bed and attempted to smooth his trunks so the bulge would go down.

"I've wanted to make out with you for so long, I guess I can wait a little bit more, but you definitely are a party pooper to stop when I'm all hot and bothered."

"And you are definitely a good kisser," Robbie said as he adjusted his own bulge. "Now, let's get out to the pool before the guests start getting ideas."

The crowd at this party was a bit larger than the one for Robbie's eighteenth birthday, although the arrangement seemed about the same.

Donavon thought that Cee Jay Seton looked a bit ridiculous wearing a big red scarf around his neck, which was obviously a souvenir recently acquired. He too was wearing surf board bathing trunks that matched Jamie's, sandals, and a 'Costa del Sol" muscle shirt. A lustful thought entered his mind. He pictured Jamie and Cee Jay doing exactly what he and Robbie had just done.

He was lost in that enticing picture when Melissa came up to him. She hugged him and kissed his cheek. "Donavon, Jamie told me about the wonderful gift you gave Robbie. What a sweet thing to do." She paused and then with a smile and wink said, "I hope he properly showed his appreciation."

Oh, my God! Donavon thought. *She knows about the ring. I wonder what else he told his wife?*

"Yeah, he sure did," Donavon stammered. Then smiling at her, he said, "He sure did show his—er—appreciation."

"That's nice. I'm so glad for both of you. My son is lucky to have found such a good boyfriend." Melissa patted him on the back and as she turned to reenter the house, Donavon detected her eyes were filling with tears of joy.

Donavon was dazed by the love and acceptance he felt by this entire family. He not only loved Robbie, but Robbie's mom and dad as well. He thought how different this family was from his own. *My mom and step-dad don't have a clue.*

This duel birthday and "going away to college" party was very similar to the one for Robbie's birthday. The guests were quite different, however. Rather than the basketball team, many of the guests were football players. And, of course, the football players had to bring half the cheerleading squad. Barbie had invited a number of her girlfriends, who, in turn, invited their boyfriends who were mostly of the preppy sort. Robbie was glad that at least Roger Pucket was there to keep him company. Roger told him that he and Judy had broken up a day or two after his party.

Again, Jamie was playing the role of official DJ and, as he put it, "security guard," making certain that no one smelled of liquor or marijuana. Cee Jay was there once again as grill-master.

Most of the guests gave humorous or sexy birthday cards; a few of the guys gave six-packs of beer tied up with a ribbon "for your first frat party", and some of the girls presented Barbie with bottles of wine with bows for "your first party at Middlebury.'

Jamie and Melissa Roberts gave Don a beautiful card and a check for $100.

Barbie presented Donavon with a long sleeve dress shirt, a green plaid bow tie, and a cardigan sweater. From Dr. Seton, Donavon received a gift similar to the one the teacher had given to Barbie for graduation. A card containing a check for $75 dollars, and four books: **The Prophet** by Kahlil Gibran, **Siddhartha** by Hermann Hesse, **Oh, the Places You'll Go!** by Dr. Seuss, and **The History of Architecture**. The last book was in place of **Leaves of Grass**, which he had given to Barbie.

Robbie admitted he didn't know what to get for Barbie, so he ending up giving her a card and a Wal Mart $25—dollar gift certificate.

At the party Robbie seemed to really lose all reluctance for dancing. He caught on quickly to slow dances, disco, and even jitter bug. He did a line dance with his father, a jitterbug with Barbie, and discoed with threesomes of both sexes unabashedly. He and Roger actually discoed together.

After the party, Donavon and Robbie were on the phone every night. Robbie wore his ring either on his finger or on the chain around his neck every day. Their telephone conversations were mostly about the crazy things the boys at the Day Camp were doing or what Roger and Robbie had done.

Once, when he knew he was alone, Robbie told Don how much he meant to him and that soon they would be able to make love. He described in vivid detail exactly what he would do. Donavon remained silent as Robbie continued the description until, all too soon it seemed, Donavon all but shouted, "Ah, Dude, I just came!" Seconds later Robbie softly said, "And so did I." They both laughed.

"Sweet dreams, lover boy."

"Good night, Don. Sleep well."

Chapter 25

THERE WAS URGENCY IN Donavon's voice when he called at six o'clock. "Hello, Roberts. Listen I just got home from Culvers Lake and have to get to my McDonald's job by seven and I'll stay until closing, so we can't talk long; but I had to talk to you. I hope I'm not interfering with dinner or anything."

"No, we're finished eating. What's up?

Something came up at the party that you don't know about."

Robbie's response of "Oh" was more of a question.

"Remember the gift I got from Dr. Seton?"

"Yeah, he gave you a couple of books and a check. He gave Barbie practically the same thing on graduation."

"It's not the books or the money that I am concerned about, Roberts. It's the card."

"What about it?"

"Well, when I read it to the gang at the party, I said it was from Dr. Seton, but he had simply written 'C.J.'"

"So? I guess he feels that now that you have graduated you could call him Cee Jay; mom, dad, and even Barbie and even I do when he's at our house."

"Okay, but there's more. He also wrote, and I'm quoting here: 'Donavon, I want you to know that you have been more than a student. If I ever had a son, I would want him to be just like you. Love, C.J.' He added a PS. 'Maybe in a way you are, though.'"

"Wow! That is really nice."

"Nice? Don't you think that's going a bit too far?"

"No. I think it's just Cee Jay being the nice guy he is. He's telling you very honestly that he really likes you."

"Robbie, I've suspected something between him and your dad since I met you at the Manor in the Poconos. I've been confiding in your dad since that incident where I nearly raped you at the Boy Scout camp, and he's told me the whole story about Dr. Seton and himself. So, here's my point: You're his lover's son. Don't you think he should be saying he wished you were his son, not me?"

"mmm. That's interesting. I wouldn't have looked at it that way, Don. If my dad and you have been confidants, my dad has also probably told Cee Jay that your dad passed away when you were very little and that your mom has since married a man that you don't get along with—that you find difficult to communicate with."

"That's possible."

"So, Cee Jay may be kind of acting as a sort of surrogate dad to you. Look, Don, I have a dad that I know loves me and I sure as hell love him. Cee Jay doesn't have any kids and you don't have any real dad, so isn't it logical that he may want to in a way kind of 'adopt' you? His PS on the card practically spells it out. And another thing: Since day one when I first mentioned you, Cee Jay has been singing your praises. 'Donavon is a great student, he's a great Boy Scout, he's a great football player.' My dad also thinks the world of you. Hell, who wouldn't want you as a son? My dad has me, and I have him. Let Cee Jay be your surrogate dad, Rice." Robbie paused briefly. "If I were older,

I'd want you as my son too, but I have you in a better way. You're my boyfriend!"

"So, you're okay with all that 'son stuff'?

"Of course."

"There is something else, though."

"What's that? Did he say that if we ever got married, he would demand to walk you down the aisle and give you away?"

"Let's not get silly here," Donavon said. "But hey, that's not a bad idea. Our getting married, I mean. Let's keep that thought in mind. But, there is something else. In addition to the check, there was something else in the card that I kind of suspected to get but didn't say anything."

"What was it? A condom!"

"Now you're just being crazy. I'm pretty sure your dad knew what was in the envelope too, but none of us said anything because we feel you should have the final word on whether or not I should accept it. It affects you too, Roberts."

"I love a mystery, but tell me...tell me. What was in the envelope?"

"Well, you will have to wait until I see you in person for that; but that does lead me to the third thing I have to tell—or ask—you about."

"I'm listening."

"I have to check into my dorm at Rutgers on Saturday. Football camp for freshmen begins on Monday. The coach wants us in the athletic building on the Piscataway campus bright eyed and bushy tailed at nine am."

"Oh. That's only a few days away. Will we be able to get together before then?"

"I've checked with the guy who will be my roommate. He doesn't have to be on campus until next week when regular freshman orientation begins the day after Labor Day. So, I'll be alone in the room for a full week when I'm not at frosh football camp. I've already discussed this with Jamie...I mean your dad...and he has agreed to drive down with his pick-up with the stuff I can't get into the beetle. Dr. Seton—er—Cee Jay will ride shot-gun with him, and if you agree, you'll ride with me. You'll be able to stay in my dorm room overnight and your dad and Cee Jay have agreed to stay in a motel in New Brunswick." When Donavon finished speaking there was silence.

"I wish that you wouldn't have to go to Rutgers at all," Robbie eventually said. "I was hoping that you'd go to the community college here for a year and then we both could go to Rutgers together."

"Yeah, I have thought of that too, but I really can't turn down the scholarships and the financial assistance packages I have for four years at Rutgers. New Brunswick isn't that far away from Sussex County, so we should be able see one another on some weekends and vacations until you finish high school. Meanwhile we can always write and keep the telephone wires hot.

"So, what do you say? Are you game for a one night 'honeymoon' in a dorm room?"

"Will you then tell me what the mystery was in Cee Jay's card?"

"Maybe I will and maybe I won't, but either way you have to come down to New Brunswick to find out."

"Only if you promise soft music, red roses, and candle light."

"You got it, buddy!"

"And one thing more. I want to dance with you naked."

"You do drive a hard bargain, Roberts, but I think I can do that. Keep it hard, I mean."

Chapter 26

JAMIE HAD IMPORTANT BUSINESS to take care of on Saturday. Robbie had gone with him to the office so that they could head over to Cee Jay's and then to Donavon's house as soon as possible. Robbie was packed and ready to spend the night in a dorm room for the first time in his life. He also couldn't wait to spend a full night making love to Donavon, even if it meant that they might not be able to be together again until the end of November when the football season would be over. Robbie had on the Docker pants that Barbie gave him. Around his neck was the chain and ring that Donavon had given to him.

The red pick-up arrived at Donavon's driveway a few minutes after twelve. Donavon already had a few suitcases, several boxes, blankets, pillows, a radio, and a large desk calendar out on the lawn. Donavon's mother came out as soon as Jamie parked his truck. She greeted the guys warmly and said how grateful she was that they were able to move Donavon to New Brunswick. She said that her husband had to work that day and couldn't help.

"I still have a chair, my computer, and a small television up in my room," Donavon said.

"Dad, why don't you and Dr. S start putting this stuff in the flat bed. Donavon and I can get those things he still has in his room."

"That sounds like a plan," Cee Jay said as he grabbed for the first suitcase.

As the teenagers went into the house, Robbie asked Don if he were excited.

"Actually," Donavon said, "I'm nervous as hell. I know I'm going to be home sick, I'm moving away from my home, my mom, my friends, and particularly you. I had to leave both jobs yesterday. It was difficult to say goodbye to the counselors and boys at the camp. Everything seems to be moving too quickly."

As soon as they got to Don's room, Robbie closed the door, and put both arms around him. They kissed longingly until Robbie felt Don's tears dripping on his own face. "I know how you feel, Don." He smiled as he wiped Don's tears with his hands. "I'm going to miss you fierce, but I'll be writing and calling you so much, you won't have time to be homesick. Now, let's do what we have to and get your stuff in the truck."

They started with the chair, which was a swivel/rocker and larger than Robbie thought it might be. When they finally got the chair down the stairs, they just left it on the lawn for the men to put on the truck bed and headed back into the house for the other items. The TV was small but still heavy and awkward, so they both had to carry it down. The last item was the computer. Robbie handled the keyboard and monitor and Donavon took the tower.

"My dad has been talking about getting a computer for our house. Mom already uses the one in the office."

"If you get one, be sure your dad gets an internet provider. We could send messages back and forth that way. Mr. Short, the business teacher, told me that typewriters will become a thing of the past real soon."

As they were leaving the bedroom, Donavon said, "Hold on a minute, Robbie, I just want to take a good look again at this room. God knows when I'll see it again. This is the place where you could say I grew up, Roberts. I hate to leave." His eyes filled with tears again, but he had a computer in his hands and couldn't wipe them away.

Outside again Don had a sad expression. Jamie said, "Come on, boy. Why so sad? A whole new world awaits you today."

Cee Jay walked around and bear hugged Donavon. "It's going to be okay, son."

Hearing the word 'son,' Donavon broke the hug. The two men faced one another and directly looked in each other's eyes. Neither said a word, but they understood and empathized. At that moment, they both knew that they were spiritually locked and would be for the rest of their lives.

After bidding his mother a fond goodbye, Donavon got into the beetle with Robbie beside him. Jamie and Cee Jay waved as they slowly drove down the driveway onto the street. It was agreed that the two vehicles would rendezvous at the first diner they would come to on route 1, just beyond the Newark Airport.

Donavon drove with one hand on the steering wheel and the other was tightly wrapped on the gear shift. Robbie held his hand lightly over his lover's. The entire trip down route 23 was passed in silence except for a few comments that Robbie would make about commercial development along the highway. As they approached the interchange in the Willowbrook area, traffic increased considerable and Donavon was forced to change gears often. Robbie kept both of his hands on his lap.

The trip to the diner from Donavon's house took almost two hours. When the teenagers got there, they saw Jamie's truck in the parking lot and pulled up next to it. "What took you guys so long?" Cee Jay said. "We have been here for over an hour."

"Bull shit! You couldn't have been here more than five-minutes," Donavon said.

"You got that right, but if it weren't for the fucking traffic, we could have been."

Donavon smiled. It was the first time he had heard his prim and proper English teacher use such profanity. "Where's Jamie?"

"He went in the diner to piss and get us coffees. I stayed in the truck to watch our precious cargo. Why don't you guys go in yourselves. I'll make a trip when Jamie comes back."

Before beginning the second part of their journey, Jamie pulled out a New Jersey Exxon map from his glove compartment and checked with Donavon on how to get to New Brunswick and Frelinghuysen Hall on College Avenue. They both said that as much as possible they would try to stay as close together as traffic would permit.

On the way to New Brunswick, Donavon became more talkative. He confessed to Robbie that he was again thinking of dropping football. "I know you said I should stick it out for at least the first year before making a final decision, but I don't know if I can last that long. I don't get any financial help as a redshirt and the competition after that is intense. Between my dual major intro classes and just getting used to university life, I don't know if I can keep up. Most of all, if I weren't on the team, I could get home more often to be with you."

It was after three in the afternoon when they finally arrived at the dormitory. Robbie was startled by the size of the six-story building. "This is a dormitory? It looks more like a hotel," he said. Jamie and Cee Jay arrived a few minutes later.

Donavon checked in at a reception desk in the lobby for his room keys and a package of instructions, campus maps, meal tickets, and numerous other items. Jamie inquired about where to park and how to unload the truck. The clerk who introduced himself as Rick Sanders was obviously an upperclassman. He told them that since it was Saturday afternoon and classes would not begin for another week, there would be no problem with parking.

"I see you are in room 420. You face the river. The elevators are to your left. I'll get a cart for you to help bring your stuff in." Rick went into a room behind the desk and emerged with a cart that he brought around to the front of the counter. He paused just long enough for Cee Jay to get the impression Rick was sizing up Donavon. "You must be here for the freshmen football camp. If you have any questions, just come down and see me. Again, Donavon, my name is Rick Sanders. I hope to see you around campus. And welcome to Rutgers, The State University."

Even with the cart and all four men carrying Donavon's possessions, it took two trips to move everything into room 420. When they were finished, they were able to relax a bit and explore the room. Robbie and Jamie first went to the window. "Nice view," Robbie said. "What's the name of that river?

Jamie, said, "It's called the Raritan."

Cee Jay explored the two built in closets on either side on the two desks, which were opposite the two twin-sized beds. "Donavon, I don't know if you picked up on it, but Rick down stairs was all over you."

"Ah, you picked up on that, too. Your gaydar is working. I thought that guy couldn't have been more obvious!" Jamie said.

"What are you guys talking about?" Robbie said.

"What Cee Jay is telling you, Robbie, is that you are going to have a lot of competition for Donavon's attention here. Rick was obviously gay to both of us."

"No way!" Donavon protested.

"Just be careful, Donavon," Cee Jay warned. "You will soon discover that in college, gay boys, particularly upperclassmen, are not as closeted about it as high school students. You'll soon get the knack of discovering them; it's called gaydar. Don't be surprised by the number of gay kids you will encounter."

"I'm hating this place more and more already," Donavon blurted.

"Just keep in mind the real reason you are here. You will get a good education for a great career, but you must keep your mind off the distractions. And sex is the greatest distraction there is. Booze and weed are the other two," Jamie cautioned.

"Jamie is a hundred percent correct about that," Cee jay interjected. "There will be many temptations. You have a guy back home who loves you and will be faithful to you. You must be faithful to him also. You may never find anyone better than Robbie, so think of him whenever you're tempted. And to put it bluntly, think with your heart and mind, not your dick."

Donavon hugged his former teacher. "Thanks, Cee Jay, I promise to follow your advice. Hey, notice I'm calling you Cee Jay."

"That's fine. Don't be surprised when I call you 'son.' Okay?"

"Well, enough of this father/son advice crap, I'm hungry. Let all go out for dinner."

Cee Jay stopped at the lobby counter to ask Rick Sanders if he could give them directions to a nice, family type of restaurant off campus but nearby. Rick suggested either the Red Lobster or the I-Hop.

Jamie drove to the I-Hop because it was closer and cheaper and he was treating. On the way he said, 'Donavon, did you know that Rutgers has a building named for Cee Jay?"

"No. Really?"

"Yeah, it's called Old Queens."

"Don't listen to him, Donavon. He's just trying to be cute with that one-liner, New Jersey gay joke. But I really do have a building named for me, but it's not here."

"Really?" Donavon questioned.

"Really. It's in South Orange. It's called Seton Hall."

Robbie and Donavon looked at one another. In unison, they both said "ha, ha" in as bored a tone as possible.

After they left the I-Hop restaurant, Jamie drove the two boys back to Frelinghuysen Hall before driving off to the Motel

6 where they had reservations for the night. "We will pick you up to go for brunch at eleven tomorrow morning. Wait for us in the lobby," Jamie said.

"Good night," Jamie and Cee Jay said at the same time.

"Love you both," Jamie added as he slowly drove off. Both teenagers stood on the sidewalk waving.

Once in room 420 both teenagers were awkward. Neither quite knew what to do or say. Robbie went to the window. As he was looking out across the Raritan River below, Donavon opened one of his suitcases; he was looking for a towel and his bath kit. He came up behind Robbie and put his arms around him. Robbie leaned into him as the older boy began licking Robbie's ears with his tongue.

"Tell me I'm not dreaming this," Robbie said.

"Okay. You're not dreaming this," Donavon whispered. After a moment, he said, "I thought your dad and Cee Jay would never leave, but now we have all night to make mad, passionate love."

He turned Robbie around, and the two young men kissed. Donavon felt a growing erection. "Now, I'm going to take a shower and brush my teeth." He started looking for his bath kit and a towel.

"mmm. I'll wash your back if you let me take a shower with you."

"Absolutely not! You know what happened last time we showered together. Besides someone may come into the shower. This is a dormitory, you know. You can take your shower when I get back."

"Okay, but don't keep me waiting too long."

"While I am taking my shower, why don't you move the beds together and put the sheets and pillow cases on."

Within fifteen minutes, Donavon was back carrying his clothes, wearing bedroom slippers. He had a large white towel around his waist. "Did you miss me?" he asked, gently kissing Robbie.

"Of course, but judging from that bulge in your towel, I'd say you missed me more." He grabbed the erection and breathed in Donavon's Old Spice and peppermint favored toothpaste.

"Go take a shower."

As soon as Robbie left the room, Donavon quickly plugged in his radio and found some soft music. From another box, he took out two votive candles, placed one on each of the two desks before lighting them. In another box, he found a vase and a bunch of plastic red roses. He placed the vase next to one of the candles. Finally, he closed the black-out drapes. He was certain the room was as romantic a setting as possible. He took off the towel that had been around his waist. He waited on the bed for Robbie's return.

"What the…?"

Donavon jumped off the bed, ran to him, and put his fingers over Robbie's mouth. "Shh!" he said. He yanked off Robbie's towel. The towel and Robbie's clothes dropped to the floor. "Remember, you wanted music, candles, and roses. So my lord, here they are. Let's dance."

They danced. Feeling their two naked bodies next to one another was blissful by itself.

They kissed. They explored one another's body from head to toe.

They ejaculated together.

On the bed, they explored each other again.

They sucked each other's cocks.

Although neither young man had ever even thought of it before, they instinctively got into a sixty-nine position. Donavon slid his tongue up and down Robbie's shaft; Robbie enjoyed running his own tongue all over Donavon's balls. At first, he wrapped one testicle in his mouth; then both. Feeling that he was about to come, Donavon pulled away slightly. Robbie softly said, "No. I want you to come in my mouth. I want to taste you." He forced Don's penis back into his mouth. Within seconds they both exploded within each other's mouths. They both remained still for several minutes as they contemplated the unutterable pleasure they had just experienced for the second time that night.

Robbie crawled back up to put his face next to Donavon's. "Wow! That was incredible!' he said.

"Roberts, you are incredible!"

"And you, Mr. Rice, are an incredible kisser."

They did kiss. They continued to kiss with Robbie on top, then they rolled over and Donavon was on top. They were still kissing when Robbie rolled over again to have Donavon on top of him. Robbie rans his hands over Don' back. He loved touching Don's ass. He ran his hand over his cheeks. Robbie slapped his lover's butt. "You know what I'd like to do now?" Robbie said.

"No. But if you want to smoke a cigarette, forget it. I don't have any."

"I want to dance again, but this time see if you can find some disco music on the radio."

While Donavon was getting a station that played club music, Robbie turned on the room light and cleared the floor of their clothes and towels. Donavon quickly found music that was fast but sultry. He began moving his hips, legs, and arms in time with the music. Robbie jumped back on the bed and crossed his legs. "Okay, baby show us what you have," he enthusiastically urged. And Donavon did. He gyrated like a professional go-go Chippendale dancer, only he was completely naked. He crotched low in front of Robbie and twirled his hard dick inches from Robbie's face. He stretched both arms out as though he were going to rub Robbie's face. He spun around and wiggled his ass and then bend over exposing his crack.

When the music ended, Donavon was a mass of sweet. His entire body was glistening. He threw himself on the bed next to Robbie who stretched out fully now.

"You are amazing, Mr. Rice. What a performance." Robbie started touching Don's wet chest. He moved his fingers around Don's navel and eventually moved to his nipples and gently bit both.

"You know what's great about our being lovers?" Robbie said smiling, "We can do things with one another, even make things up…do crazy things like you just did, and we can find out together how to do new things that we both like. And we never have to be embarrassed or afraid."

Robbie put both legs at Don's side and knelt over him. He positioned himself so that bending down he could kiss Donavon. They did kiss, but then Robbie sat back to gently run his hands through Don's hair. He gently ran a finger slowly over Don's face, ending by circling his mouth. Don reached over and grabbed Robbie's cock which had grown hard again. Robbie raised himself so that he was kneeling not sitting on Don. He wanted Don to play with his dick more. He reached behind himself and made a fist around Don's shaft. He got a thrill out of feeling it swell in his hand. He began swinging Don's cock over his ass, then running it into his crack. He loved the reaction that he felt in doing this, and he sensed that Don enjoyed it too.

"I bet you would like to put that big piece of bologna in my ass, wouldn't you?" he coyly whispered in Donavon's ear.

"You betcha I would," Donavon said with a silly smile.

"So would I. I'd like you to penetrate my virgin ass, if I can do the same to you."

"Okay, by me," Don said, "as long as we are both slow and easy with one another."

"I think that sounds exciting, but not tonight. We'll probably need a ton of lubricate. What's it called, KY, or something?"

"Next time I'll have it,' Donavon said. "Also gives us something to explore together. I do so totally want to be in you, Roberts."

"Me too," Robbie said. He slid down Don's legs so that their dicks were side by side and he began rubbing them together. After a minute or so Donavon took over the action, and soon they both felt the release of semen streaming from both of their cocks onto Donavon's chest and Robbie's pelvic area. Robbie made sure that both cocks had released their last drops of cum before he began playing with it. He made sure he had a big glob of cum on his finger before putting it his mouth. "mmm, good," he said smiling. Donavon grabbed Robbie's shoulders and pulled him down. They exchanged a very warm kiss before swallowing.

They lay in silence for a short, ecstatic time before Donavon said, "My God, did we just do it three times?"

"Yep, and I bet my big Eagle Scout loved it every time."

"Confession, Robbie. Before we met in the Poconos that time I averaged whacking off about once a month. Since then about once a week, thinking about you. Never three times in one day. Hell, within a few hours!"

"We should take a shower. Think you could control yourself with both of us showering at the same time? I promise to use a shower far away from you."

"Yes, but you'll have to wash your own back," Donavon said.

They both put on slippers and wrapped their towels around their waists to go the short distance to the men's room and showers.

When they got back to the dorm room, Donavon noted that it was after one AM. He turned off the light, and they cuddled up on the bed. They were exhausted but felt a sense of great release. Donavon put an arm around Robbie to hold him close.

In the dark, Robbie said, "So what's the mysterious thing that you found in the envelope that Cee Jay gave you on your birthday?"

"Oh, that. Well, it's not so much a mystery. It's really something that I want to discuss with you and get your opinion on, but I'm really too tired to discuss it now. It really can wait until tomorrow morning. Okay?"

"Sure. I'm too tired to give my opinion on anything right now. Unless you want my opinion on loving you. That's something we don't have to discuss. My opinion is definitely a resounding 'Yes, I do love you Donavon Rice.'"

"Good, because I love you too, Robert Roberts."

Hours earlier, across town, in a Motel 6 room, Jamie Roberts and Cee Jay Seton had finished their own love making, but both felt a little restless and didn't feel ready to go to sleep.

Cee Jae started to get dressed again. "I want to walk around a bit outside. Get some fresh air. You may join me, if you wish."

"Sounds good. I need some exercise and fresh air too."

"I'll wait for you on the walkway." Cee Jay left the door ajar.

Outside Cee Jay was holding onto the rail around the second story of the motel outdoor walkway that all the rooms led out to. The temperature gauge on the bank building across the street read 85 degrees, but the stifling humidity made it feel much hotter. Cee Jay immediately began to question his decision to leave the air-conditioned room, but the moon was shining brightly amid puffy clouds.

Jamie closed the door with the key. He put his hand over his lover's. "Penny for your thoughts, but I bet I know what they are anyway. You're thinking about my son and Donavon over in that dorm room."

"We are getting to the point where we can read one another's minds." Cee Jay said.

"I think they are so young, so innocent, so inexperienced. Right now, they may think they are madly in love, but how long will that last, Jamie?"

"I guess only God knows the answer to that question, Cee Jay. You may think they're too young, too inexperienced, that it could never last. But look at me and Melissa. We were even younger. I was only seventeen when we had to get married, but we were deeply in love and right for one another. Two kids and nineteen years later, we are still together. Yes, Robbie and Don are going to have their problems, their share of doubts; but they will share their joys and experiences, and grow up together. Their lack of experience can be a shared blessing."

"More than anything, I hope they succeed. Life is not easy, and being gay certainly doesn't make anything easier."

"They will have to follow their own paths. All we can do is love them, pray for them, and give them as much help and encouragement as we can. Speaking of which, has Donavon said anything to you yet about your very generous offer of giving them the keys to your man cave to use on weekends and whenever they wish? I know that you gave Don the keys on his birthday. Has he said anything to you yet? He told me that he wanted to discuss it with Robbie before accepting your offer."

"Yes, he told me the same thing."

Jamie chuckled. "Well, if we see Robbie wearing that chain with both the ring that Don gave him and a key around his neck tomorrow, we will know the answer."

"You know, Jamie, there is a great deal of irony here. I almost think of their lives in a way as a kind of continuation of our own story."

"Yeah, I guess you could say it is a sequel."

Author's Note

How did Jamie and Cee Jay Meet?

READERS OF *HE'S FACING Sex Evolution* may enjoy reading *Greenwich Village Tales*. Also written by Chuck Walko, it is set largely in Greenwich Village, New York City. These "Tales" are narrated by none other than Cee Jay Seton, whom you have met in *He's Facing Sex Evolution*. You will learn how he met Jamie Roberts "before Robbie was even born." Two full chapters are devoted to Jamie, who is also mentioned briefly throughout *Greenwich Village Tales*.

The fictitious 'La Bar' is a neighborhood, gay hang-out. Here, Cee Jay meets a number of homosexual men, each of whom represents a typical personality in pre-Stonewall society. They include teachers, intellectuals, atheists, Roman Catholic priests, bisexuals, and male prostitutes. Their stories are humorous, serious, and even tragic; but all of these characters may be among us even to this day. True love, however, is not experienced in "Tales" until the surprising end.

Greenwich Village Tales should appeal to people of any sexual orientation. The reader should be forewarned, however, that this novel contains controversial topics and some explicit sex and language.

About the Author

CHUCK HAS BEEN A teacher, administrator, real estate appraiser and broker. He has taught students in grades seven through twelve in suburban and inner-city schools as well as private preparatory schools. He also has been an adjunct professor at several colleges and universities. "The 'real-life' stories of my students have always been my source of inspiration," he says.

A native of New Jersey, he now lives in sunny Arizona. "My passions are life-long learning, reading, writing, travel, physical fitness, and, of course, Diamondback baseball."